Ildland

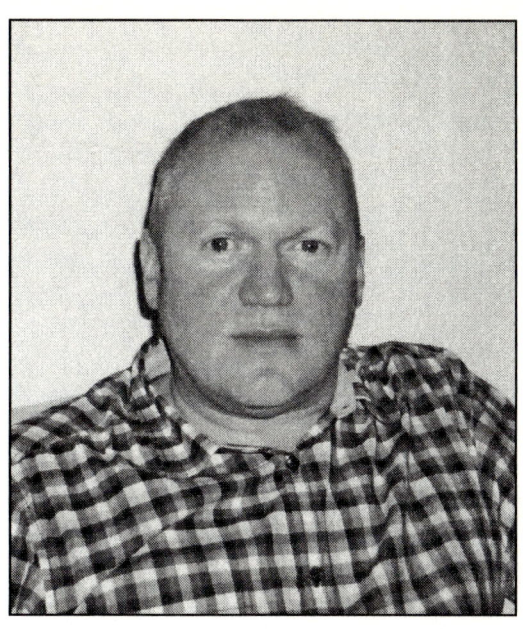

A natural dreamer, part of me – Hugh A. Henderson – has always wanted to create a fantasy world, full of adventure, love and hope.

It has been a long time coming, but here it is.

Everything in this book has never been far from my heart – It is with this in mind that I dedicate it to my son Dion, with the wish that all his dreams may come true.

Ildland

Hugh Henderson

Ildland

Olympia Publishers
London

www.olympiapublishers.com
OLYMPIA PAPERBACK EDITION

A CIP catalogue record for this title is
available from the British Library.

ISBN: 978-1-84897-056-4

This is a work of fiction.
Names, characters, places and incidents originate from the writer's
imagination. Any resemblance to actual persons, living or dead, is
purely coincidental.

First Published in 2010

Olympia Publishers
60 Cannon Street
London
EC4N 6NP

Printed in Great Britain

To Dion,

May all your dreams come true

CHAPTER ONE

The wizard Jeremiah lived in a kingdom that was once a very happy one. Unfortunately, though, as the great King John advanced in years, conflicts of all kinds had started in the land.

The enemies of the king were becoming more and more powerful.

They were led by ferocious gangs of rebel knights.

Nobody knew how many members these gangs had, but there were enough of them to place morbid fear into the hearts of the many good people of the king.

Even with all the troubles in the kingdom it had to be said that Jeremiah was renowned for his love of life and even more for his love of Adam.

Adam was an ordinary boy who had befriended the wizard when he was very young. He was the son of a blacksmith who made shoes for the horses of the king, and his regiments.

Adam lived with his father in a place called the Valley of Friends; his mother had died of a fever when he was only three. The valley was a quiet, secluded place not far from a small township.

All in the area knew of the troubles in the land, though it

seemed strange to them as King John's castle was nearby, and from these people he deserved nothing but respect.

Sadly, for Adam, these troubles were to change his life on one terrible day that he was never to forget.

Enemies of the king had ridden down into the valley early one morning.

They had made out that they were travelling men on a great quest overland.

Adam's father had spoken to them for a while whilst working. He had checked the shoes of their horses and even helped with directions out of the valley to the next town.

Just as their business seemed complete, one of the six men spoke out against the king.

A fight started and Adam's father, who was a fine swordsman, did not back down.

Four of the men had fallen before he was finally struck down.

Adam had tried to help his father, but had been hit, very hard with the flat of one of the men's swords, hard enough to have bloodied his nose.

Adam managed to get back to his feet and go to his father's side, as the two remaining men rode away from the scene leaving their slain friends.

Jeremiah had wandered into the valley later that day and saw Adam with his father's head resting in his lap; he was crying softly.

Jeremiah rushed to aid Adam, comforted him (he had grown

very close to the boy in all the years he had visited the blacksmith) and agreed that very day to take him in as his own.

When all the arrangements had been made with the king, Adam moved from the Valley of Friends and into the small woodland cottage of the wizard Jeremiah.

CHAPTER TWO

"Wake up… wake up!"

Adam had been shocked out of his sleep by the hissed command of his friend.

"What is it?" asked Adam, still half asleep.

"The time has come for us to leave this kingdom," said the wizard.

"But where will we go?"

The wizard did not answer Adam's question, he merely motioned for the boy to get dressed.

Adam was soon ready, then he and the wizard left the woodland cottage that they had had so many happy times in.

As they made their way through the woods the wizard told Adam he had received news that both the king and queen had been slain in their beds earlier that night.

"The rebels are victorious," he said gravely. "This is no place for us or the children of this land. I was a friend and humble servant of our great king for many years… I suppose we both knew that this would happen one day."

The wizard did not speak for a moment, then he sighed and added, "Come quickly, the others will have heard my call. We must get to them before any are captured by those accursed rebel knights."

Adam wanted to ask who the others were, but thinking better of it due to the solemn tone of his friend, he just followed through the ever densening woods.

Adam, although a little frightened by the night-time flight, was soon lost in his own thoughts.

It had been several years since the death of his father – all the while the rebels had become more and more organised in their fight against the king.

The royal armies had been scattered throughout the kingdom in various battles to save the sovereignty.

Both of the king's fine sons were killed by his enemies and his supporters were at a loss to know who would take over from him.

There was no certainty as to who it was that started the troubles (though Jeremiah had his ideas) and many fell in with the rebel knights as they feared both for their own lives and the lives of their families.

The moon had moved position in the sky a good deal before Adam and Jeremiah were finally out of the woods.

They were now running through long grass – it was so long that Adam wondered how his friend could possibly see where he was heading, given that he was very short.

As previously he opted to keep up without question.

It was almost dawn; their pace had slowed tremendously, when they broke cover from the grass.

They came upon a sight that Adam could hardly believe.

They were on a cliff-top and before them a vast expanse of water shone like a giant sapphire as the first light of sun came.

He looked to Jeremiah and the wizard said simply, "The sea."

He let Adam look for a few moments and then gently took his hand.

"We must go."

He was pointing to a small gap in the cliff-top rocks.

Adam followed.

There was a path just beyond the rocks and the two of them started to make their way down to the sea-shore.

The path was very steep, causing both of them to make each step a careful choice.

When they reached the yellow shore Adam was allowed, once again, to marvel at the sea.

Jeremiah had described the sea to him in great detail and had always promised to bring him. As he stood, with the sea breeze blowing on his face, tasting salt on his lips he realised nothing could have prepared him for it.

"Come, we must find the others."

Adam followed the wizard in to a cave hidden by shadow from the cliffs. They travelled a little way in and then entered a much larger cavern.

Much to Adam's surprise a group of children he knew from the township were sitting either on the soft sand of the floor or a rock formation off to one side.

There were nineteen children in all (most a few years younger than his twelve): nine boys, nine girls and one older girl, older than he was.

Adam had come to know her only by sight – she was of noble birth and her name was Evangeline.

Evangeline was, in fact, the same age as Adam – something he found out later from Jeremiah.

Her hair was black as night, her eyes as green as the grass, her skin fair and her mouth cherry-red.

Her beauty gave her the appearance of a young adult and it was only when she came close that the radiance of her youth glowed from within.

Adam turned to ask the wizard what this was all about.

Jeremiah had his index finger over his lips indicating that his young friend should stay quiet.

"Come."

At the command from the wizard (and without a word) the group gathered up their few belongings and then followed Adam and Jeremiah out of the cavern.

They made their way to the shore, stopping close to the sea.

Jeremiah stood before them all, water lapping at his feet.

He then spoke in a voice that Adam found hard to recognise as that of the friend he knew so well.

"Our king is dead. I have called you to this place to tell you that we are all to leave this kingdom. You have been chosen to join me on the most fantastic of journeys."

The wizard's words were burrowing their way into the very souls of his young followers.

"We must leave because the rebels are throughout the kingdom now. They will be part of a rule that leads with the hardest of hands. They are men of the very worst kind. They will turn father against father and mother against mother. They want power for the sake of power. They will take a life for the sake of taking a life. I believe they will carry out unimaginable evil to achieve their goals. I believe them to be followers of Cornelius!"

It did not take long for the wizard's words to sink in. The whole of this group knew their parents had been strong supporters of King John. If not of noble blood they certainly believed in noble standing.

A few of the younger children began to cry, for it was now clear that the death of the king would bring about the deaths of their parents.

The rebels could not be seen to allow anyone to threaten their new order.

"Come children, do not weep," said Jeremiah, "for I know you suffer great loss now, but I also know that you will all be re-united with your parents one day. There are many worlds in our universe; we are to go to one of these now and they shall be watching over us all from another."

These words had fallen softly on the ears of the young and had dried their tears – they had no reason not to trust the wizard for they all knew of his goodness.

They also knew that if these rebels were followers of Cornelius it would be unwise to stay – his legend was known to them all.

"Up on the cliff! Can you see?" Adam's cry brought to their attention a small band of men on horse-back. They were trying to find a way down.

The wizard turned to face the sea.

His arms raised skyward, the wizard began speaking in a language unknown to any of the group.

They could only watch in awe as the new dawn sky turned back to black.

The wind was picking up and it was soon obvious that a violent storm was brewing. Adam and Evangeline worked hard to keep the younger children calm even though fear had drained all the colour from their own cheeks.

It had often been said that Jeremiah was the most powerful of all wizards, but before now the group had only ever seen him do conjuring tricks for their amusement.

There was more to come. Much, much more.

A huge clap of thunder shook everything around to the foundations, forks of lightning lit up the sky – and then the rain started.

It was freezing rain, the kind that chills to the core.

Adam watched as the band of men on the cliff-top tried desperately to control their mounts.

One man had come too close to the edge – he was thrown from his horse and plunged down the rock-face. Adam looked away in horror. He did not see where the man landed.

The sky was jet now, the lightning illuminating the faces of the terrified children.

Adam was sure it was in the minds of everyone in the group to run, but the depth of the magic rooted them where they stood.

There was a new sound now, like an enormous cloth being torn.

Jeremiah, still speaking in tongues, was waving his arms around in a furious fashion as the sound got louder.

And louder.

And louder.

It was Evangeline who saw it first.

"Look!" she shouted, over the howl of the storm and the tearing sound.

All watched as, somewhere far off in the horizon, a jagged line of white light was making its way towards the shore.

"SHOW US THE WAY!"

The cry of the wizard was now louder than anything else.

"SHOW US THE WAY!"

The jagged white line of light was above their heads now. It was so bright that they had to shield their eyes.

Adam watched through the slightly open fingers of his hands which were protecting his eyes – two lightning forks met the wizard's upturned palms.

Jeremiah stood and seemed to grow as his whole body glowed with an incredible power, his arms extended out in front of him – The light from within crackled out from his finger-tips.

He was building a bridge, seemingly made just from light. It arched way above the water, going to a place that none of the group could see.

The wizard stepped on to the bridge and gestured that they should follow.

Evangeline took the lead and Adam brought up the rear to ensure they all got on.

It was such a strange feeling, his feet could feel nothing yet his weight was supported.

As they walked further along the bridge Adam checked to see the whereabouts of the men on the cliff.

None had travelled down to the shore. Most were now standing by their horses looking out to where the group were.

The storm was quickly subsiding.

As Adam turned his back on the land he had once loved so dearly he was aware that with each step he made, a little of the light behind him would flicker out.

He was now also completely dry.

As their journey progressed, each member of the group was finding it harder to control the sense of excitement within them.

The journey on the bridge was long.

It was also the cause of some strange and, at times, saddening sensations for Adam.

Many things he did not understand flashed before his eyes. There were young ones who looked like him and not at all like him, all at the same time.

He watched as fighting men fought battles of a scale where it seemed there really could be no winners.

He saw his mother and father together again – he felt a great happiness as well as a huge sense of loss at this vision – he so wanted to be with them.

For the whole of the time the journey lasted Adam wished it would never end and he was certain that the others, including Jeremiah, must have felt the same.

A short while after Adam had seen his parents together again a night-time darkness fell upon them.

There was no feeling of fear amongst the group as they were all sure that the wizard would never allow any harm to come to them.

It was just before any doubt could have crept in that a small circle of light could be seen at the end of the tunnel of darkness.

As they made their way towards it the light took on the shape of a doorway.

Within moments they had all travelled through and were then met with the sickness you feel in your stomach when you plummet downwards.

It was as if they had all jumped from the cliff they had travelled from down to the shore. The air pushing upwards as they fell at a breath-taking speed made their hair stand on end.

At one point it had actually blown Jeremiah's long, pointed hat clean off, but Adam caught it with both hands and held on to it tightly – he knew his friend would hate to be without it.

Gradually their speed slowed. Adam watched as one by one, each member of the group hung suspended for a moment and then disappeared.

Panic was just beginning to seep in to him when it came to his turn; he felt as if he had hit a cushion. A large, deep and soft cushion.

Then, he dangled helplessly, legs flailing about, until he was sucked in to something that made him feel like he was going down into a whirlpool.

Before Adam could see where he was, his eyes were forced shut and the voices of his parents were in his head. They were singing a lullaby, a song he could recall being sung when he was very young.

The sound was so sweet that he did not want to open his eyes – instead, he drifted off to sleep.

****

Adam awoke from his dreamless sleep feeling more alive than ever.

He was aware of the warm sunshine on his face and he found he was lying comfortably on the greenest of grass.

He sat up to take in more of his surroundings and was left almost breathless by what he saw, such was the joy it filled him with.

The group had come to rest on the brow of a hill and down below, as far as the eye could see, was the most beautiful countryside.

There were meadows and woodlands, dazzling displays of flowers and any spaces were filled with the same emerald green grass he sat upon.

"Ah! Adam, come and join us." The wizard's voice was cheerful.

Jeremiah was sitting just a little way away, circled by a small group of the children, who were giggling merrily.

The rest were playing a chase game led by Evangeline who, in this place, looked even more beautiful.

"Jeremiah, I can say in all honesty that I am quite the hungriest I have ever been!" Adam exclaimed as he joined the group.

Adam had learnt a very regal way of speaking for one as young as he. Most of his ways had been taught to him in the years he had lived with the wizard.

He was a tall boy now; at times he made his short and ruddy friend rather resemble an elf. His poise was good and his stride would soon develop the confidence of a well trained soldier.

The wizard had conjured up the most marvellous of breakfasts: there was cold chicken, crusty bread, a good selection of fruits and a glorious juice made from crushed berries.

All the time that he ate Adam thought of the things he had seen on their journey across the sea.

He had many questions to ask his friend.

The children were now getting up to join in the games being played with Evangeline and it was not long before he and the wizard were left alone.

"Adam," said Jeremiah, "there are many things we have to discuss about this place and there are also many things that you must learn before you are to become king."

"King?" Adam asked, feeling the kind of dread one feels when they have done something wrong and know they are about to be found out.

"Yes, Adam, king," the wizard repeated. "Listen to my tale and you will understand for there are many times when the purity of a child's mind allows greater understanding of those things even a wise man cannot."

Adam, now taken in by the wizard's words, sat back and listened intently as the story of times past unfolded.

CHAPTER THREE

There was not one person in the kingdom knew whence the wizard Cornelius had come, but his arrival, and that of his followers, had brought with them all the powers of darkness.

The land that these simple people had known was turned in to a bleak, desolate place in which there was no telling day from night, a place where there was much suffering, a place where the blackest of magic cut deep in to the frightened hearts of the people.

It was true that everybody feared Cornelius, but it was also true that some people were willing to overcome those fears to claim back the right to rule their own destinies.

One such man was Johannes.

He was a descendant of the great explorer Per.

Way before Johannes was born Per had set out on a journey overseas that had been commissioned by the king of his homeland. There was great excitement amongst the people of his town for all, very often in their dreams, wanted to sail the high seas.

There had been many months of preparation with careful selection of crews for the two voyaging longboats and the gathering of supplies for the journey (including ale and strong bottled spirits for the hardy seamen).

There were the plans for the proposed route, taking in Per's knowledge and the experiences of the other sailors. The main point, for Per anyway, was whether to take his wife Gitte.

Gitte (who was with child) managed to browbeat Per into letting her sail.

Then, the evening before the departure finally came, the king threw the most elaborate street party.

All the toils of the day finished early and the farewell celebrations commenced.

There was music and dance, good food and wine – a banquet on a scale that this small town had not seen for a very long time.

The celebrations went on into the early hours of the morning and included, in some corners, silent prayers to the gods asking that the journey be safe for all involved – especially the headstrong Gitte.

When dawn's first light broke, and the last of the singing was in the farthest reaches of the town, Per led the first of the longboats out of the harbour, to what was almost a silent goodbye.

The journey they had embarked upon was to take several weeks and would change history for a place that became known as Vandland.

****

Johannes had heard the tale of the great journey many times and it was this for him, plus the courage of his own convictions, that made him lead the fight against Cornelius.

He gathered together a band of men of his kind and fought many battles throughout the land.

They swooped down from the hills and slew the followers of Cornelius in bloody sword fights.

They crept in and out of the mine encampments killing the evil men of Cornelius in their beds, freeing the workers until the last battle was to take place.

The men of Johannes had advanced upon the castle of Cornelius.

For days arrows flew through the air into the bodies of good and bad alike; swords cut in to chain-mail, daggers drove through hearts, oil poured down the castle walls burning the soldiers below.

However, for every man that died, two more would come and join Johannes in the fight to rid the land of Cornelius.

These men had remembered the courage of their forefathers, they remembered how the people of this land had welcomed the people of their own.

For Johannes, he remembered that it was Cornelius who had killed all of his family before taking him as a slave labourer.

It was in the hearts of these people to be warriors, as it was also in their hearts to protect those who had given them so much in their new homeland.

The castle gates had been smashed and finally Johannes was in.

At his side was a young warrior whom he did not know, and as they fought their way through what remained of the army of Cornelius, Johannes could only marvel at the strength of this incredible soldier.

Johannes, the young warrior and a small group of men had entered the inner chambers of the castle.

It was there they came before Cornelius himself. He stood clutching a volume of magic bound in black and gold.

It was from this and with a mere click of his fingers that he summoned hideous winged creatures, with claws of steel, setting them upon the men of Johannes.

Somehow, they fought them off.

Men of shadow appeared to fight for the wizard Cornelius; they moved so swiftly and appeared unbeatable, for a while it seemed that the battle was lost.

It was then that a cry of defiance came from the young warrior.

"Begone! Begone demons of the dark!"

Form his sword came an unbelievable power; he led the group in a swath through the shadow men cutting through them as if they were not armed at all.

He now stood before Cornelius.

"By the powers of darkness!" Cornelius began to chant, "I summon…"

Before he could finish the young warrior screamed, "No! You are finished, Cornelius! You are to have no more power over these people!"

His sword raised in both hands above his head, the young warrior commanded, "Begone!"

He stepped forward and, as he had with the shadow men, cut the wizard into a thousand tiny pieces.

Cornelius did not die as a mortal would; he became a ghost-like apparition as the attack began and simply disappeared slice by slice.

His howls of pain rang around the castle until all that was left was the book that had been in his hands.

The young warrior scooped it up and turned to the others.

"Johannes, you must lead your men out of here!"

Even as he spoke the walls were crumbling from within.

Stone by stone the castle started to fall.

The earth below was opening up to swallow the castle floors.

Johannes led his men from the inner chambers and through the corridors of evil as the stones tumbled down around them until they, at last, were outside.

It was only then that he realised that the young warrior was no longer with them, and as the castle was razed to the ground he, along with the others, saw the black sky beginning to turn back to blue.

****

"What has all this to do with me?" asked Adam as Jeremiah's tale drew to its end.

"Johannes," said Jeremiah, "was a man of many talents, Adam, though he did not become king for it was not of his choosing. He, as were all of his family men, was a warrior and explorer. He elected a man he deemed to be more suited, the man called Holgar. Holgar, out of respect for Johannes and the people of Vandland past, named his first son John, as it combined the languages of both peoples. John the First was a forefather of our own great king and Johannes was a forefather of your own family. Your own father was himself a courageous warrior in his time."

Now, Adam understood his destiny in this new land.

"Evangeline is to be your queen," said the wizard, obviously happy with his choice.

Adam had just one question for the man he had for so long regarded as his father and his only true friend.

"If all of this is so, Jeremiah, then tell me who was the young warrior?"

"Some lives are eternal, Adam, but even those with the greatest of gifts need to rest for a time. That time will soon be coming for me."

The wizard finished all of his explanations by reaching deep in to the cloak that he always wore drawing out a book of magic bound in black and gold.

CHAPTER FOUR

Billy had had an absolutely awful day. It was his third day at his new school and he was already longing for half-term.

The story for him always seemed to be the same; he would just about be settled somewhere when his father would announce another move.

The latest move had brought him, his mother and father to the small town of Chiggleworth. His father was to take charge of a vast building project about a mile outside of town – one of those retail parks that Billy hated so.

"Isn't this a lovely place?" his father had asked when they had driven around the town on the day of their arrival.

"I don't suppose it will be for long," a miserable Billy had muttered under his breath.

So, here he was just a few days later with a black-eye, a torn blazer and clutching his broken glasses, shuffling up the path to the cottage that was (for the moment anyway) home.

"What on…?" his mother began as Billy stepped through the back door into the kitchen.

"I fell…" Billy lied; "I'm sorry, Mum."

"You were fighting! You're doing it again! What will your father say?"

"I don't care," is what he wanted to say, but instead came, "I said I'm sorry."

After much fussing his mother helped clean him up.

Over tea his father treated him to stony silence, after his usual lecture.

Once the table was cleared Billy decided to have an early night.

He went upstairs, leaving his mother with needle and thread sewing his blazer pocket back on and his father with a scowl on his face, nose buried in the local paper.

****

As he made his way to school the next day it seemed to Billy that his father would never understand him.

He was actually a clever boy, but he did find it hard to make friends.

Many times, due to his appearance – his taped glasses certainly would not help today – he was thought of as a swot.

When he refrained from answering questions in class his teachers thought him slow and any bullies would tease him about his lack of intelligence.

All of this would lead to fights which, unfortunately, Billy usually lost due to the fact that he was hopeless at fighting.

It was as he had finished pondering on this that Billy decided not to go to school.

Just one day to himself, he thought.

No bullies, no stolen dinner money, no torn blazer, no school, no school, no school!

If Billy had said this aloud his voice would have been very

loud indeed.

His tie and blazer removed he headed into town.

His father had been right, it was a lovely place.

There were cobbled streets, quaint little shops and a small market place.

He stopped in one of the shops and bought himself some chocolate and decided to visit the fields outside of town before his father built his retail park all over them.

"Billy!"

The voice of Jenkins was a hissed sneer.

Billy stopped at the door of the shop.

Jenkins was there with his whole gang of cronies: Jones, Atkins, Smith and Thompson.

"That's my favourite," said Jenkins, as he snatched the chocolate from Billy's hand.

"Give me that!"

Without thinking, Billy had lunged at his tormentor.

The worm had finally turned. The force of his blow had knocked Jenkins off his feet.

Everybody stood, shocked for a moment, until Jenkins shouted, "Get him!"

Billy knew he had no chance against them all and barged between Atkins and Smith.

The few that had spoken to him at Chiggleworth Middle had all told him to avoid these boys, but as always, the bullies decided to come after him.

As he ran down the street Billy remembered all the places he had been and how trouble had followed him relentlessly.

The beating he had received from Jenkins and his gang the

previous day was down to the fact that Billy had spoken to the wrong girl.

He had bumped into her, quite literally, outside one of his classes. He had apologised, feeling silly at his own carelessness.

She just smiled and, for a moment, held him fixed to the spot with her gaze. She had the greenest eyes that he had ever seen.

It was not that much later when Jenkins had set upon him.

Billy had seen the girl again, very briefly and had merely said hello.

She smiled again and passed him by.

He had walked on feeling happy with himself for it seemed quite probable that he had made a friend.

He was making his way down the lane towards home when he met the gang.

"Billy!" Jenkins had shouted.

The gang stepped out from their hiding places.

"So, what do you think you're doing talking to my girlfriend then, eh?"

Billy doubted that the very charming girl that he had ploughed into was in any way connected to Jenkins, but rather than argue he said, "I'm sorry, I didn't know!"

"Well, you do now!" And with that, the whole gang set upon him.

Billy's cause had been helpless.

Remembering, all too vividly, the events of the day before, Billy carried on running.

He could hear the snarls of the gang behind him and the cussing of passers-by as Jenkins led the chase with no respect for the people on the street.

Billy turned in to a narrow road, then again a little way down and to his horror realised he had entered a dead-end alley.

The wall confronting him was far too high to climb and as he turned to face his foes he could feel the tears of frustration welling up in his eyes.

There was nowhere to run.

They were now all at the top of the alley. All that stood between Billy and them was a couple of dustbins, some boxes, a few bags of rubbish and on the opposing walls two doors that appeared to be rusted shut.

Instinctively Billy carried on backing down the alley.

Jenkins kicked a box out of the way and growled at Billy, "Now you're for it!"

Billy was pressed against the back wall when it happened.

He was shoved away from the wall, as if hit by an outward opening door and a pure, brilliant white light lit up the whole of the alley.

He became aware of somebody, legs astride, standing over him.

The boy was tall, much taller than Billy and dressed in a style of times long gone by.

He wore a hessian tunic, calf length trousers made of a rough cloth, a wide belt and he carried a staff.

He lifted Billy to his feet and stood between him and the gang.

Jenkins was afraid, but far too proud a bully not to order the attack.

"Let's get both of them!"

The boy stepped forward to further the gap between the bullies and Billy.

Now, Billy could see that, for some reason, he had found an

ally.

Jenkins was side-stepped, the boy moved very quickly in his sandaled feet and with his staff he swept Jenkins' feet from under him.

Jenkins fell heavily in to one of the dustbins – his squeal of pain was, almost, music to Billy's ears.

The rest of the gang were dealt with in quick succession through a series of sharp raps from the staff.

Jones was winded due to a blow to the stomach; Atkins fell after being hit on the top of the head; Smith and Thompson were evaded skilfully as the boy moved between them, then tripped them both in a single move causing them both to land, with a bump, on their behinds.

Whilst the gang were trying to regain their senses the boy grabbed Billy by the arm and pushed him through the entrance that appeared in the wall where, originally, he had lost hope and prepared for a real pasting.

Seconds later the town of Chiggleworth had disappeared from view as a heavy oak door, rather like the kind you would find in a castle, slammed shut behind them and the wall became whole once more.

CHAPTER FIVE

Billy was now totally confused.

He had seen the oak door disappear, followed by the alley wall, only to find the door was back – it was, however, standing with no support in the middle of the brow of a hill.

He and the boy were (or so he supposed) on the other side of it.

Before he could say anything the boy said; "You have made the journey between worlds!"

Billy found he could walk around the door.

"This doorway is now shut," said the boy.

He guided Billy around it again, then took his staff and pushed the door – it fell flat on the grass.

"Where am I?" asked Billy.

Looking around him he could see nothing at all except bleak, cold countryside.

"This place is called the Hill of Beginnings – it is part of a kingdom named Ildland. Come, Master William, we have a good journey ahead of us and should really begin as soon as possible."

"How did you know my name?" Billy's tone probably showed he was feeling the first real signs of alarm.

"I probably know more of you than your own self. If you will be so good as to follow me I will do my best to explain. My name is Joseph; I am the last known descendant of our first king, Adam. I am pleased that we are finally able to meet."

With his last statement Joseph offered his hand to Billy.

Billy took it and felt some comfort in its firm grasp.

"I'm pleased to meet you too," Billy said, doing his best to emulate his new friend's regal manner.

"Here," said Joseph, "I managed to salvage this. Put it on for it will become colder soon."

Billy took his blazer (it had been knocked from his grip in the alley).

Somehow, Joseph had managed to tuck it under his belt as they had travelled through the door, but his tie and school bag were gone.

"I'm ready." Billy had buttoned himself all the way up.

"Come then," said Joseph and began to lead the way down the hill.

****

The journey was a much more fraught affair than Billy could ever have imagined.

It seemed to grow colder by the minute and on at least three occasions there had been downpours of freezing rain.

The whole land seemed barren, all the trees and flowers appeared to have died, and he had become so hungry that he expected to fall to his knees at any time.

In between the rain, there was the intolerable hunger pangs and wondering what on earth he would tell his parents as to why he was so late home.

He was also trying to listen, with as much respect as he could muster, to the stories Joseph was telling him.

Joseph spoke of a place called Vandland, a wizard called Jeremiah, King Adam, the beautiful Queen Evangeline, another evil wizard named Cornelius and a book of magic.

Billy's mind was a blur, his feet throbbed and he was starting to intensely dislike the place he was in (after all, he had not asked to come here) and to add insult to injury the rain had soaked him through.

If there was one thing that Billy hated, really hated, was being wet.

The sky had turned completely black – Billy had never remembered a night as black as this back home – with just a couple of stars making for poor visibility when Joseph's words trailed mid-sentence.

He stopped and listened.

Then, they heard sound of hooves.

"Quickly, hide here!" he ordered Billy.

The path they had been on was lined with dead trees and coarse bracken.

Billy did as he was told and hid behind some particularly dense bracken with Joseph at his side.

The sound of the hooves came much closer.

Flaming torches were now lighting up the landscape in an eerie fashion.

Joseph motioned for Billy to lay down flat as the torch-light parade drew even nearer.

As it came into full view Joseph placed his hand firmly over Billy's mouth to stop him crying out.

Billy lay, unable to make a sound, looking on both mortified and mesmerised.

It was a kind of procession, but it was a procession of evil.

There was a man at the front clad totally in black – if it had not been for the torch in his hand it would have been hard to have seen him at all.

Behind him a score more, all dressed in the same uniform of black chain-mail, armour-plated vests and a variety of nasty-looking weapons about their person.

Between these men and another group was a line of people tied in single file; their hands were roped in front of them and their feet shackled making escape impossible.

All the prisoners held their heads down as they made their way along the path.

This is the how the line went on, groups of prisoners surrounded back and front by the black knights.

At one point a man in the middle of a group of prisoners fell; the man behind him tried to help him up only to feel the lash of a whip across his back causing him to cry out.

The man who had fallen managed to drag himself back to his feet and, without a word of complaint, carried on.

It had taken at least half an hour for the procession to pass and only then did Joseph take his hand from Billy's mouth.

Billy had nothing to say anyway.

The tremors that had coursed through his body the whole time he had watched the master and slave procession had numbed him into silence.

They stayed where they were until the last flickering light of the burning torches had gone.

Joseph then turned to Billy and said; "I think now, Master William you will begin to understand the plight of this land."

They both got to their feet and dusted themselves off.

Before he made his reply Billy felt something from within him that he had never felt before; a steely conviction replaced the tremors of earlier, he felt as if he were here for a purpose.

He did not fully understand what was coming from his very soul, but he turned to Joseph and, as William, spoke.

"This injustice will stop, Joseph. I promise you now, this injustice will stop."

Joseph allowed himself a smile.

"Come," he said, "we have a way to go yet."

He and Billy got back on the path and recommenced their journey into the night.

CHAPTER SIX

It was much later that night when Billy and Joseph came upon the ruins of what had once been a great castle.

The moat was now completely dry and the remains of the drawbridge had dropped diagonally into it.

Joseph clambered down a little way into the moat and offered a helping hand to Billy.

Once they had made their way to the bottom, Joseph led Billy under what remained of the drawbridge.

It was here he pushed some bracken aside and stepped into a concealed entrance.

Billy followed him in and helped rearrange the bracken so that the entrance was hidden once more.

They were now immersed in almost total darkness.

"Put your hands on my shoulders," Joseph said, "I will lead the way."

Billy did as he was told and for a while they moved, very awkwardly, through the black corridor.

Joseph turned to the left, catching Billy by surprise and causing him to fall headlong.

"Ouch!" he exclaimed as small, sharp stones dug in to his palms.

He heard Joseph scuttle off, returning within seconds with a flaming torch in his hand.

"Come quickly, this way!" Joseph's whisper was one of urgency.

Billy scrambled to his feet.

They made their way into another corridor.

"Are you hurt, Master William?" Joseph's voice now showed genuine concern.

"No. I'm fine," Billy replied, picking at his palms and trying not to wince.

"We can have no torch where its light could be seen, for there is no way of knowing who may come by."

Billy took in their new surroundings.

They were in a place that rather resembled a mine-shaft (at least how he imagined a mine-shaft would be); beams supported a roof of hard earth and equally placed slats.

The passage had a low roof though, making walking only possible by stooping.

"This will take us to the inner chambers of the castle," Joseph explained. "We made this tunnel ourselves as a route in and out that does not involve us moving above the ground until it is absolutely necessary."

It was not too long before they had come to what Joseph had referred to as the "inner chambers".

Billy noted that they were actually in the dungeon of the castle.

There was a group of children inside, varying in ages from (he guessed) five up to his eleven.

There was a girl who particularly caught his attention.

She stepped forward and extended a graceful hand.

"Master William," she said, "at last you are here."

Billy took her hand – the warmth which came from it was almost overwhelming.

"You…" Billy was once again, transfixed by the beautiful green eyes that had got him into so much trouble with Jenkins.

"Yes, me," she laughed softly, and then added, "My name is Alicia."

"That's a very pretty name," Billy complimented trying hard not to come across as some sort of stammering buffoon.

"Master William," Joseph interjected, "let us offer you some refreshment and a change of clothing. We shall all need some rest for we have much to do in the next few days."

Billy was introduced to the rest of the group, even though they all knew who he was, something he still found a little disconcerting.

Billy was then able to wash (some fresh water had been warmed over the fire in the middle of the dungeon and placed in a bowl); receive a change of clothes and be fed.

All the time that he spent with the group, before he finally slept, he was unable to take his eyes off Alicia.

He made small talk with them all in an attempt to divert his attention; and he had made them all laugh when he offered his school uniform to the fire.

Still, though, her face made his heart beat fast and then filled his dreams until he had begun to forget all about bullies and school and home.

****

"If there is evil in your heart, the book of magic will find it and tempt you. It is a volume of incredible powers, it can blind you to yourself or help you create the best of things, its powers are far greater than that of any wizard, but a wizard who has the book, well…" Joseph trailed off.

Billy had asked Joseph to go over some of the story he had heard the night before, again.

"So, whether good or bad, the book can you give you anything you want?"

"Yes. But there is so much more to it than that - I am not sure how to explain it."

"Is the book in the kingdom now?"

"Yes it is. The wizard Cornelius has it."

"But, I thought Cornelius was dead," said Billy, puzzled.

"Unfortunately, as it seems with all great evils, they can be destroyed for a time, but rarely die forever."

Joseph continued, "The book can be used as the doorway between worlds. Nobody can really say for sure where it came from or who created it. My father was betrayed by one of his own men – the evil in his heart meant that Cornelius was able to get to him through the book. The Black Knights, or Army of Darkness as we call them, scattered the people of the land and Cornelius was in a position of power again. When this, the home of my forefathers fell, the revenge of Cornelius was complete; my father, the king Nikolai, had managed to hide some of us children in the woodlands nearby."

"Where is your father now?"

"I wish I knew. He disappeared not long after finding us the hiding place in the woods. I brought us back here hoping that we would at least be safe as it seemed the last place that anyone would look."

"How long have you been here?"

"Two years."

Looking at the group Billy could only marvel at their achievements.

The sense of unity and his belonging made him feel the same surge of strength as he had after the passing of the Black Knights – it seemed Joseph had felt it too this time.

The two boys smiled a smile of encouragement at each other.

"I have something for you," said Joseph.

He got to his feet and walked to the table in the corner of the room.

He brought back a long package wrapped in the same, rough hessian material as their clothing. He handed it to Billy. Billy accepted the package.

Inside was a sword in its scabbard; as he took the hilt Billy's hand tingled.

Joseph then produced a small book from the pouch that hung from his belt.

"This should answer any other questions you may have," he said, passing the book to Billy.

Billy nodded, then opened it and read the inscription on the very first page.

The paper was yellowing (rather like some of the old books you would see in a museum) and the handwriting had been written with a quill pen.

It said, "To Adam, with all my wishes for your health, happiness and good fortune – Jeremiah".

CHAPTER SEVEN

Once Billy had started reading the book of Jeremiah it became apparent that the good wizard, was a man of extraordinary vision.

Each page not only contained words of wisdom, but also was able to form vivid pictures in the mind's eye.

All the things that Joseph had told him were somehow in its pages, though for Billy, it seemed to tell him so much more.

He was able to understand more of the book of magic; the book had no name, it just was.

It was indeed a symbol of absolute purity or absolute evil; Jeremiah's book was a guide to all things including the use of the book of magic.

At no point during his reading of Jeremiah's words did Billy feel there was an order to do anything; they simply suggested possible courses of action.

As the words within its pages drew to a close, Billy knew that one day, he had no way of telling when, there would be more pages of script added.

For the moment though, there was a warning aimed directly at Billy.

It was upon reading this that Billy felt the first genuine shiver of real fear run down his spine.

It was just at the point when he had finished reading that Alicia approached him.

"How are you today, Master William?"

"I am very well, thank you," he replied.

"I know you have been chosen," she said, her tone becoming quite sad, "Please tell me, are there more dark times ahead?"

Billy could not lie to her.

"Yes," he said, "there are more dark times coming. It will take all the courage we have to try and overcome them."

Her eyes lowered for a moment and it looked as if she might cry.

Billy touched her hand in some small attempt to comfort her.

She looked into his eyes and again her question implored him for an honest answer.

"Is my brother going to die?"

"Your brother?"

"Yes, Joseph. Has he not told you that he is my brother?"

"No. He has not."

Billy looked closely at her features and could now see the resemblance to Joseph.

Before he answered her question he had to think very carefully; the book of Jeremiah had contained a warning that, as yet, he did not fully understand.

As he replied he felt the fear gnaw at him again and, although this fear was greater than any he had ever known, he remained calm as he spoke. "I do not know. We will all, at some point, have to pray for our lives. Cornelius knows we are here, I am sure. My very arrival will have upset the balance of things.

"I know you have many plans to make with Joseph," Alicia said and turned away from him.

Billy felt, as she walked away, that he had told the most dreadful of lies. His problem was that he really did not know the answer to her question.

As he contemplated he turned the small book over and over in his hands.

Joseph would soon return from his hunting trip, and then they could begin to make plans together.

On the table in the corner of the room Billy's glasses were crushed under the weight of a pot that Alicia needed to place down.

All the time that he was reading Billy had not even noticed that he was not wearing them.

It was only on finding them later that Billy could see that he had finally broken away from his old self.

The group ate well that night – Joseph's hunt with two of the older boys had been good – and they did need to start early the next day.

Once the others were asleep Billy and Joseph packed some necessary provisions whilst taking stock of the few weapons they had for the battles ahead.

CHAPTER EIGHT

The group got everything together very quickly that morning with Joseph leading them away from the ruins of the castle just after first light.

As they made their way, in the opposite direction to that by which they had arrived at the castle, Billy fell in line next to Joseph.

The two boys who had been on the hunt with Joseph brought up the rear of the group.

Billy looked along the line and wondered how on earth they were going to win in their pledged battle against Cornelius.

Most of the smaller children would be of little use in a fight so, as far as he could see, there was only Joseph, Alicia, Luke and Jack (the boys who hunted with Joseph) and himself to bring about the fall of the evil wizard.

Not only was this prospect daunting to Billy's mind, it was made all the worse by the sense of duty to protect the younger ones, of whom there were fifteen in all.

For a good while the group moved in silence, all lost in their own thoughts.

Every now and then Billy afforded himself a glance at Joseph.

His warrior friend seemed to have a face that had been carved in stone. Billy wondered how much Joseph had understood of the book of Jeremiah, for he had made a point of not introducing

Alicia as his sister.

Again, the one warning of the book sprang into his thoughts and Billy had to try very hard to keep his fear from showing.

He patted the pouch that hung from his belt in the vain hope of gaining some reassurance.

In the cold light of day this, the journey he had read about and the plans he had made with Joseph, seemed like the most foolhardy thing that he had ever been involved in.

****

They had walked for most of the day, only stopping briefly for lunch, when Joseph finally gave the order for them to rest.

The group had wandered from the main paths and into the cover of woodland some time ago.

"We shall camp here for tonight," Joseph said. "Alicia, go with Luke to collect some fire wood, but do not travel too far from this spot."

They were in a small clearing shrouded on all sides by trees – it was a good place to camp as any fire would be offered the maximum of cover.

It was not long before Alicia and Luke had returned and they had been able to start a small fire.

The whole group had to huddle closely together to benefit from the warmth.

They ate a meal that was much less hearty than the night before – they were all too tired to eat a lot – then Joseph helped Alicia with the bed-rolls so that the young ones could sleep.

Once the younger members of the party were settled Joseph organised sentry duty.

Looking up through the trees at the moon they listened as Joseph instructed (using the tree tops as a guide) where the moon would be before they were to switch over.

All the watches would be longer than any of them would have preferred, but there were too few of them to have any choice in the matter.

Billy was to take the first watch with Alicia – Joseph had explained that this would be best as they were the least experienced. Any enemy attack was much more likely to come later in the night.

Luke and Jack were ideal for second watch as they were both used to night hunting.

Joseph was to take the last watch and although he would be alone, he had the advantage of daybreak coming after an hour or so into it.

As the others settled in amongst the rest of the group, Billy moved with Alicia to a suitable vantage point.

The fire was now just a pile of red glowing embers, so both wrapped their blankets around their shoulders in a cape-like fashion as protection against the increasing chill of the night.

They sat, back to back, and watched.

Few words passed between them though each was aware of the discomfort of the other in this situation.

Billy held his sword in front of him and when their watch had passed, he was grateful of the chance to sleep with the young and ensured Alicia was not far from him.

****

It seemed as if he had only been asleep for minutes when Billy was awoken by screams and confusion all around him.

Taking his sword in his hand he scrambled to his feet to see what was happening.

The group was being attacked by huge birds. They were of a bat-like appearance, but with the beaks and talons of eagles.

They were able to drop straight out of the sky, talons extended, then, just as easily, hover or carry themselves back upwards to avoid the swords of Joseph, Jack and Luke.

Billy, to his utter dismay, also saw two of the young ones had already been taken up through the trees.

They were held by the shoulders in the steely grip of the creatures' talons.

One of the birds came too close to Billy who, with a vicious swipe of his sword, brought it crashing to earth in a bloodied heap.

Alicia struck a second down with a well aimed arrow from her bow.

Many of the creatures were falling now, but for every one that fell, another came just as quickly to carry on the fight.

As the bloody battle continued to rage more of the children were taken up into the air.

It was a fair while later that it stopped.

The moon was lower in the sky now and the five exhausted warriors were alone. All of them were bruised and bleeding from the attack.

Billy stared helplessly up at the sky and could just make out the last of the birds swooping off into the distance, its distinctive shrieks almost impossible to hear above the cries of the child it carried.

Billy looked to Joseph, the face of his friend showed no signs of emotion at all until (this was something Billy never expected to see) a large tear welled up in one eye and coursed down his cheek.

This was followed by more, then more and still more.

Joseph dropped to his knees as the first sobs shook through his body.

Alicia stood by her brother's side and placed a gentle hand on his shoulder.

She began to cry also.

There was no shame in this now – Billy, Jack and Luke let their own tears free.

The bodies of twelve or more birds lay about them, and yet their efforts to save the children had amounted to nothing.

The tears they shared were all but finished when they heard the laughter.

It was an evil, demonic laugh that could have struck fear in the heart of the most courageous of men.

It acted like wind on the trees, causing them to sway and their leaves to fall.

It jeered at them in its mirth at the horror they had seen.

This was the first introduction Billy had had to Cornelius.

With incredible anger he shouted at the sky, "I CURSE YOU CORNELIUS AND BY MY SWORD YOU SHALL DIE!"

And with that he brought his sword down on one of the winged creatures drawing its last breaths.

The bird would have died shortly anyway (the wounds it had already received would have seen to that), but the single hack that took of its head gave Billy's curse more credibility.

The laughter faded away abruptly.

Billy turned to the others and said, "You are all braver than any I have ever known." He then added, mainly for the benefit of Joseph, "This was not the fault of any of us."

CHAPTER NINE

It had been hard for them all to get any rest after the attack. Each of them were lost in their own individual nightmares and all most likely feeling that the rest believed their mission was a lost cause.

Perhaps it was these unspoken feelings that somehow now kept them united.

After all, it really did seem that there was little else to lose.

When they had finished a rather meagre breakfast they recommenced their journey.

Joseph seemed to know the land they were now travelling through quite well, and it was this that struck a curious note with Billy.

"Have you travelled here before?" he asked.

"No, I have not. It is just with the things that I learnt from my father and from the book of Jeremiah it is as though..." Joseph thought hard for the right words. "It is as though I can feel the way to go."

"I have learnt a lot from the book also," said Billy, "but, it has not taught me how to be a guide."

Joseph allowed himself to accept Billy's compliment on his usefulness to the group.

Billy knew that Joseph still thought he was partially to blame for the events of the night before.

Realising how close they had become Billy didn't like to see Joseph hurt.

"Master William, you know, between us all, we might win this thing yet!" Joseph replied with all the cheer he could muster.

They shared a knowing smile, and the strength of the bond between them raised the spirits of the rest of the group as well.

****

The five came to rest that night, still in the cover of the wood.

They were all tired due to having so little rest the night before and being so hungry.

"How much longer do you think we will be travelling through these woods?" Billy asked Joseph.

"I am hoping we will be out of them some time tomorrow. We need to get food and more water as soon as possible. We must also try to get as good a rest as we can tonight."

The group ate what was left of the provisions they had brought and Joseph arranged guard duty exactly as it had been the previous night.

At least this would be easier now as there were so few of them left to protect.

Alicia and Billy arranged their blankets in the same fashion as before, and then sat back to back.

This night they had stopped in a clearing barely big enough for them all and the small fire they had built.

Billy looked upward and all he could make out clearly was tree branches; the sky was hardly visible at all, just trees and blackness.

If it were not for the light coming from their camp-fire he would not be able to see his hand if he held it up in front of his face.

The night was like a heavy veil around them all, and, thankfully, passed without incident.

CHAPTER TEN

The five made good progress during the early part of the next day (the benefit of a better night's rest had paid dividends) and after about three hours of walking they broke cover from the woods.

They were now on a plateau of grass beyond which there was every indication of a steep drop.

Joseph motioned for the group to stop.

They all sat on the grass, not too far from the first line of trees of the wood.

"Let us rest here for a while," Joseph said, "I wish to tell you of some of the things to come. I think you, Master William, may be more prepared for possible events than I."

The look exchanged between Joseph and Billy passed unnoticed with the rest of the group.

Billy said nothing. He merely nodded and waited for Joseph to continue.

"We are headed towards a place called the Black Mountain," Joseph began, "and it is here that valuable lessons may be learnt in how the destruction of Cornelius can be brought about. To get to the mountain we must first pass through an area named the Valley of Truth. This is the only way to get to the mountain and is the place where all of our inner strengths will be tested to the limit. We must all do what we can to stay as one, for this is the time that we could become weak and, if we weaken, our mission could easily fail."

"I do not understand," said Alicia, "what is the Valley of Truth?"

"Master William, perhaps you will try to explain?"

Billy agreed to Joseph's request and did his best to make his words as clear as possible.

"Imagine if you were really, completely exposed to your true self. The seemingly purest of souls could have a very dark side and if it were released may make a challenge to the best in you. It is almost as if..." Billy felt himself floundering, "as if you were able to split the two sides into separate beings, good and bad could then go to battle with each other."

Before Billy was able to say anything else Alicia asked, "So, there is a chance that the evil in you could win?"

"Yes," Billy said in total honesty. "I suppose, in some ways, it is like the book of magic – only it won't actually give you anything. It could just take an awful lot away."

Billy could see his words (something he had hoped would not happen) had frightened Alicia, Luke and Jack.

Joseph was doing his best to look unmoved.

Billy knew that Joseph, in fact, was probably the most frightened of them all.

Remembering the warning in the book of Jeremiah made Billy's flesh crawl, again.

Billy decided to try and lighten the mood.

"As long as we keep our wits about us," he said; "everything should be fine. We will be able to get food and water in the valley and in less than two days' travelling time we will be at the foot of the Black Mountain."

The mention of food cheered them all, for now the pangs of hunger within them had become audible.

As if on cue, Billy's stomach rumbled very loudly.

The whole group laughed, causing Billy to blush.

"We had best get on our way," he said, allowing himself to smile.

They all got on their feet and made their way to the edge of the plateau.

****

The way down to the valley was a lot easier than any of them had expected.

Once they had discovered it, a path that looked as if it had been cut in to the rocks for walkers, made short work of the decline.

Joseph led the group down, whilst Billy brought up the rear, checking all the way for any signs of further attack.

None came.

When they had reached the bottom they all looked back up at the slope. It seemed to reach far into the sky.

Billy noticed, for the first time since he had been in the kingdom anyway, that the sky was blue.

The rest saw this as well now.

"My, it really is quite warm here," Alicia smiled at Billy.

The valley was wide and flanked on either side by steep, high inclines. This, coupled with the path they had just taken in to the valley, meant the most sensible way forward was straight ahead.

"Look," said Billy, pointing to a mountain in the distance.

Even though it seemed small from where they were standing there was no mistaking the outline of the Black Mountain.

"It would be hard to lose our way now," Joseph joked.

A feeling of well-being was washing over the group.

It was not long before they came across fresh water. Its source was somewhere high up on the incline to their left and by the time it reached the valley it was a reasonably wide stream. The stream looked as if it ran the length of the valley, with trees on either side that bore delicious-looking fruits of varieties that Billy had never seen.

The group drank deep and then filled their near empty flasks.

They picked some fruit from the trees and spent some time chatting amicably in the warmth of the valley.

By the time the first signs of darkness came the group were feeling tired.

They had travelled a long way and were once again in need of a good night's rest.

Luke and Jack had hunted, managing to bag a couple of rabbits.

Whilst they had been gone the others had made up a fire between some trees and the stream.

After the skinning had been dealt with (a task which made Billy feel a little sick) they all sat around and waited for their supper to cook.

The night sky was clear and the stars caused patterns of light to dance across the stream.

As they ate Billy found himself looking more and more into the eyes of Alicia.

Her smiles were those of unashamed happiness.

Luke and Jack laughed loudly, like two young boys who had not a care in the world.

Only Joseph remained strangely subdued during the meal

(something which Billy had noticed, but was guilty of trying to ignore).

It was late before they finally settled down to sleep, all of them now too tired to worry about anyone doing sentry duty.

It was something that did not seem necessary here and shortly after covering up they were all asleep.

****

Billy woke in a cold, sticky sweat.

His sleep had been troubled with the most horrible of nightmares. He sat up and looked at the faces of the others. In the light of the fire all seemed to resting peacefully except for Joseph.

He was thrashing about under his cover. Billy could see that his face was also beading heavily with perspiration.

Billy was concerned for his friend and wanted to wake him, but knew that it could be dangerous to wake anyone from a nightmare.

So, instead, he sat for a while until it seemed that Joseph was resting without trouble.

Billy got up, walked to the stream, where he knelt and splashed some cool water on his face.

As he was returning he heard, though barely recognised, the voice of Joseph.

"Where have you been?" came the demand.

"I only went to the stream. I woke up. I had some sort of nightmare. I…"

Billy could now make out Joseph clearly and stopped mid-sentence.

Joseph's face was almost grey in colour. His eyes pierced Billy with a stare that could turn a man to stone.

"Let's get back to sleep," Billy tried suggesting.

"I give the orders here!" Joseph shouted.

The others were now waking up.

"What is it? What is wrong?" Billy asked, trying to contain his fear.

Joseph was moving toward Billy with his sword drawn.

"Joseph, what are you doing?"

Joseph turned his attention to Alicia and pointing at Billy growled, "He is a traitor!"

"Joseph," Billy could see that there was no reasoning with him, but continued, "why should I want to betray you? I am here to help you."

"Then tell me, where did you go?"

"I told you, to the stream. I..."

"LIAR!" Joseph bellowed; "You want to become the leader! I am the true destined king! I will not let you take what is rightfully mine away from me!"

"Joseph, stop this!" Alicia gave her voice as much force as she could muster.

Joseph ignored her and gave Billy the order, "Draw your sword!"

"No, Joseph, I shall not."

"Draw it!"

Jack made a sudden lunge toward Joseph.

Joseph swung his sword, slashing Jack across the stomach.

Jack reeled backwards clutching the wound; he just about

managed to stay on his feet with the aid of Luke.

"Joseph, remember the warning! You can fight this! Remember the warning in the book of Jeremiah!"

Billy was sure that this would get through.

"Jeremiah! That old fool! Ildland is my kingdom! I am destined to rule it! I alone! Now, draw your sword or I shall cut you down where you stand!"

"There is nobody here but us, Joseph. Look around you. We are all your allies. Please, think of what you are saying."

Joseph's command cut in to Billy's words.

"Draw your sword! We shall see who is true to his word!"

"Do as he says." Alicia's voice sounded very small and now her eyes were filling with tears.

Billy looked at her helplessly as he went to where his sword lay; he drew it from its scabbard and turned to face Joseph.

"I do not want this, Joseph. I will fight you because you want me to. You, though, must give me your word on one thing. If you kill me, you must let the others go."

"They are all puny and worthless to me, thus, their lives are of no consequence. You have my word. The word of a king!"

Billy held up his sword and spoke to the others; "Stay out of this. You can do nothing to stop it."

Billy moved forward, both hands on the hilt of his sword.

The fight began with a mighty clash of blades.

Joseph's skill and power had Billy immediately on the defensive.

Billy took a few steps back to regain his composure.

The fury of Joseph's next attack had Billy countering swipe after swipe.

On each contact the clatter of metal on metal rang loudly in Billy's ears.

They circled.

They clashed again.

Billy was tiring, his heart pounding fast with the fear that realisation was bringing; he had no chance of winning.

A few seconds later Billy was cut badly on his left arm, then gashed across the legs.

The next swing narrowly missed Billy's head and in avoiding the blow he stumbled on to his back losing his grip on his sword.

Joseph stood over him with his own sword raised above his head.

Billy felt as a gladiator would be waiting for the "thumbs down".

Joseph smiled down at Billy.

Billy was too exhausted now to attempt any defence.

Just as he was expecting to die Billy heard the sound.

A dull thud.

The look on Joseph's face was one of both surprise and pain.

His sword fell from his hands and he tumbled to the ground.

An arrow was embedded, deep, between his shoulder blades.

Luke stood with Alicia's bow in his right hand.

Jack was sitting holding on to his stomach, blood still seeping through his fingers.

"I could not do it," said Alicia, "somebody had to."

Joseph was lying on his side, all the madness gone from his face.

His eyes moved slowly round making contact with them all,

before looking between those of Billy and Alicia.

"I am truly sorry," he managed to say. And then he died.

CHAPTER ELEVEN

The funeral service for Joseph was a simple one.

Billy and Luke dug a shallow grave (by hand mostly) then wrapped Joseph in his bed-roll.

Alicia tended to Jack's stomach wound, unable to watch the preparations.

Once everything was ready Billy could only think to say the words of the Lord's Prayer as a goodbye to his friend.

When he had finished he stuck Joseph's sword in the ground at the head of the grave.

They left Alicia alone for a few moments to say her own prayers.

By dawn's first light it was all over and, in the saddest of moods, the group left Joseph to his final rest.

****

It was Luke that spoke first later in the day.

Alicia and Jack were slightly ahead of them when he said to Billy, "You should not feel too badly about what happened. It was not your fault."

"I know. I just wish it did not have to be this way. He was my friend."

"He was my friend too. When Alicia gave me her bow I wished that it could have been anyone but me."

"Alicia gave you her bow?"

"Yes. She was ready to use it. She knew what Joseph was doing was wrong. She just could not do it."

Billy looked ahead to where Alicia was helping the weakened Jack with walking.

"That must have taken incredible courage," Billy said, "to even think it."

They fell silent again.

The group had to stop much earlier to camp than they had the night before as Jack's condition had slowed them considerably, so Billy thought it best that they completed the journey to the Black Mountain the next day.

Billy helped Jack with his injury and also paid some attention to his own.

"You try to rest as best you can, Jack," Billy said as he re-dressed the wound; "it will take a little time to reach the mountain tomorrow."

"Thank you, Master William. I do feel tired. I am sure I will be better by tomorrow."

Jack slumped into Billy's arms; he was asleep.

Billy lay Jack down as gently as he could.

Fresh blood was beginning to stain the clean dressing already.

Luke and Alicia made a fire and, as they had done the night before, they ate rabbit.

"Save some for Jack." Billy wanted to ensure that he could be fed when he woke.

"How is he?"

It was the first time that day that he had heard Alicia speak.

"Not good," Billy answered; "He is still bleeding quite badly. The cut is deeper than I had imagined it would be."

"The events of last night have certainly taken their toll," Alicia said sadly.

Billy could see the pain in her eyes and wished so much that he could say just one thing that might comfort her.

"Perhaps we should have a watch tonight," Luke suggested. "We may be safer."

Alicia shook her head.

"Any attack on us will only come from within. For all we know Cornelius is watching us now and laughing at what happened. Joseph warned us about becoming weak, yet it was he who weakened first. If one of us is awake, we will all have to stay awake for we cannot even trust ourselves here."

Her words had become full of bitterness as she fought desperately to control the coming tears.

Billy drew her to him and she cried, with very little sound, for a long while.

When she had finished both Billy and Luke did their level best to offer some words of encouragement.

She accepted them with good grace and, at one point, even managed an attempt at a smile.

She then checked on Jack and told them it was time for them all to sleep.

****

Jack was no better in the morning. His dressing was soaked with blood and his speech had become incoherent.

Billy fed him a little of the meat they had saved and got him to take some water.

He changed his dressing after bathing the wound at the edge of the stream.

Jack was almost incapable of coordinated movement so the journey time was much slower than Billy had hoped it would be.

It was late in the afternoon before they were at the foot of the mountain.

As they had come closer to it they became more and more aware of its vast size.

Standing at the foot of it they discovered its strange composition.

The rock (if it was rock) of the mountain was completely smooth. There was no way it could be climbed.

Billy and Luke left Alicia at Jack's side (he was now unconscious) to get a closer look.

"How do we get up?" asked Luke. "We cannot possibly climb this."

"I think," Billy answered, "we have to get in."

"In?"

"Yes. In."

Billy reached in to his pouch and took out the book of Jeremiah.

"Help Alicia with Jack. The book will tell us what to do."

Luke did as he was asked.

They left Jack propped, rather ungraciously, against a rock at the foot of the mountain.

Billy flicked through the pages of the book.

"Have you found anything?" Luke asked after a few minutes had passed.

"No. I do not understand this at all," Billy said, "The book has been a kind of guide to get here, yet there seems no way of getting in. I feel sure that we have to get in."

Billy studied the book a while longer.

"Master William, look at this."

Alicia was running her hand over the surface of the mountain.

"There is some sort of pattern running around the bottom. It is not very clear."

Billy walked over to where Alicia was crouching and stooped to join her examination of the pattern.

There was a definite structure of carved symbols, all faint with age.

"What is it? Is it some kind of ancient writing?" Billy queried.

"I am not sure," Alicia answered.

They followed the carvings to the rock that Jack was supported by.

The book glowed, suddenly hot in Billy's hand.

"This is it!" Billy exclaimed; "Luke, help Alicia move Jack!"

The two managed to get Jack to his feet, which was hard work now as he was a complete dead-weight.

Billy heaved the rock to one side and dusted off the surface behind.

There was a curious grid-like shape cut into this point, much clearer than the rest as it had been protected from the abrasive elements.

Billy looked at the book and watched, amazed, as the same

grid showed from within its cover.

Billy placed the book against the carving and found it fitted as a key would fit its intended lock.

An area of the mountain's surface began to open inward. The sound it made was painful to the ears.

It squeaked, groaned, creaked and squealed for a while until there was just enough of an entrance revealed for them to squeeze in.

At this point the movement and the symphony of rotten noises stopped.

The book was ejected from the rock. Billy returned it to his pouch.

"I suppose we'd better go inside," said Billy, not really relishing the prospect.

He went over to help Luke with Jack, as Alicia was just about done in by his weight, and they went through the opening.

Before any of them could see what was going to happen, the doorway slammed shut.

They were left in total darkness.

CHAPTER TWELVE

The dark did not last for too long.

A torch lit up from its mount on the wall to the right of them and revealed a stairway ahead.

The stairway was walled on both sides and was quite narrow.

Since the way behind them was now sealed the only way to go was up.

"Take the torch," Billy said to Alicia, "You had best lead the way."

Alicia took the torch and they began to make their way up the stairs.

At first the course the stairs took was straight, then they spiralled, then they went downwards as if going back on themselves and then they went up and up and up.

The ascent was hard work for Billy and Luke as the unconscious Jack's limp body offered no cooperation at all, making every step an effort.

The group had to stop many times so that Billy and Luke could rest; all of them were beginning to feel that the stairs were a maze that really led nowhere at all.

They were wrong.

They had been about to give up hope when they could see the last of the stairs led to a passageway, at the end of which was a door.

Billy and Luke hauled Jack over the last step feeling very proud of themselves for having managed to get to the top at all.

Alicia held the torch and they all stood in its flickering light wondering what to do next.

"Should we knock?" Alicia asked.

"It would be good manners," Billy answered.

Still, they hesitated.

"Can you manage Jack on your own for a second?"

Luke nodded and Billy made toward the door.

He rapped on it with as much confidence as he could muster.

No reply came; instead the door just swung open.

Billy returned to help Luke with Jack and the group made their way in.

As had happened previously, once they were through the doorway, it closed behind them.

They stood in a room that was lit by torches spaced between huge stone tablets. The stones were of a different composition to the rock and ran from ceiling to floor.

They were covered in ancient writings.

At the far end of the room was an altar, and behind this hung a drape that was decorated with a variety of crudely formed images.

The images looked – if studied from left to right – to be telling a story of some kind.

Next to the door they came through was an empty torch mount and it was as Alicia hung the torch that they all noticed that the door had no latch.

"There is no way to get out," said Alicia, trying not to sound scared.

"I feel sure there must be," Billy replied, though he was also alarmed to see no way to open the door and recalled that the first doorway had also sealed behind them.

How were they going to get out?

As if she knew exactly what Billy was thinking Alicia then said, "I am not sure that I like this at all."

"We had best get Jack to the altar," Billy said, trying to get them all to think of something else. "At least he may be able to rest properly there."

They put Jack on the altar. For the first time in a while now he looked vaguely comfortable.

Billy placed his bed-roll under Jack and said softly, "You will be fine my friend, you will be fine."

They stood for a while in silence.

Billy was the one to break it.

"Luke, could you help me with the drape?"

The drape moved fairly easily, some sort of system was obviously in place to allow it to travel smoothly, although this could not be seen from the floor.

They exposed another door which had a latch.

This time Billy just opted for opening the door and peering inside.

This room was much smaller. Its only furnishing was a throne that was placed in the middle of a plinth which was against the opposing wall.

The room was lit by two torches mounted on the wall either side of the throne.

"Stay with Jack," Billy said to Alicia and Luke. "I shall only be a moment."

He took a step inside the room. He moved, very slowly,

towards the throne.

"Master William!" the dual cry from Alicia and Luke did not stop the door shutting before he could get out.

Two enormous bolts slid into place ensuring his friends could not get in.

Billy tried in vain to move the bolts.

He could hear Alicia and Luke pounding on the door from the other side as well as frantically trying the latch.

"Try not to worry!" he shouted. "I will figure out a way to open it!"

Billy was not at all certain how he would do this as he had used all the strength he had to slide the bolts, but to no avail.

Before he had time to really ponder upon his predicament a voice behind him said, "Not without my help, young man."

CHAPTER THIRTEEN

Billy turned, ready to draw his sword.

The pounding on the door had stopped (albeit down to his assurances) and the quiet made it feel as if his friends were a million miles away.

There was now a man sitting on the throne.

His hair was black and very long, worn casually in a pony-tail that fell over his left shoulder. He was dressed totally in black and would have had quite a menacing appearance were it not for the sparkle in his eyes.

"Welcome, Master William," he said and smiled.

The smile was warm and put Billy at ease until the man made a move to get up.

The speed at which Billy drew his sword surprised them both.

The man stayed seated, the smile on his face getting broader and his eyes sparkling all the more.

Billy, still doing his best to look threatening, found this a little off-putting.

"Who are you?" demanded Billy.

"Why, Master William; I was rather hoping you would have guessed. Oh, well, such is my vanity. My name is Jeremiah."

"Jeremiah? Oh, goodness! Please, let me apologise for my

rudeness."

Billy gave a half-bow, then deciding that this made him look even more foolish; he replaced his sword in its scabbard and offered his hand for the wizard to shake.

The wizard extended his hand and Billy tried to make his grasp firm and confident. This, alas, was to no avail.

His fingers merely passed through the hand of the wizard leaving him gripping at nothing but air.

Billy jumped back.

"Are you a ghost?"

"No, no, young man. Not a ghost. I am just not yet whole."

"Whole?"

"Whole."

"Oh."

The wizard laughed.

It was a friendly laugh, not at all mocking and Billy found that he could not help smiling himself.

"Come, sit by me, Master William; after all that has happened to you I do admire the fact that you still have the will to fight."

The wizard fell silent for a moment and Billy could see that he was trying carefully to fathom out how to begin.

He began with a question.

"Master William, do you understand your choosing?"

"Choosing?"

"Yes. Do you understand why you are here?"

Billy had heard the word chosen in reference to him very few times; he had, on the other hand, read it in the book of Jeremiah, many times over.

"I believe that I have been chosen because I am an outsider."

The answer Billy gave was not to the wizard's satisfaction.

"And?" Jeremiah prompted.

"Well," Billy started, "the first King Adam was new to this world. He built the kingdom of Ildland on a dream and the dreams of the children who were brought here with him. To return to the dream an outsider must begin everything again."

Billy looked to the wizard who, again, was waiting for him to say more.

"As an outsider I can see everything for what it is. Good for good; evil for evil. My opinions here are all my own. They cannot be shaped. That is why…"

Billy faltered for he did not want to finish his sentence.

"Why what?" the wizard asked.

"That is why, given the opportunity, Cornelius will try to kill me."

"You," said the wizard, "are a very astute young man. Yes, it is true; he will try to destroy you. I, however, must see to it that you bring about the salvation of Ildland."

The wizard finished on such a triumphant note that it gave the impression that the deed was already done.

Billy wished he could share Jeremiah's enthusiasm.

"How can I win against Cornelius? I only have Alicia and Luke still able to be of any real help…" Billy asked doubtfully.

"You will not be a few! You will be many! And not just children! Come now, have some faith! You may feel as if you have lost some battles, but you will win this war!

Billy pondered the wizard's words for a moment and then, in a very small voice, asked, "Are you going to help us?"

"I will guide you all I can and, once I am whole again, I will be part of the crusade."

"And, when will you be whole again?"

The twinkle in the wizard's eyes had gone. In a rather sheepish tone, as if he hoped that this question would not be asked, he said, "That, I must confess, I do not know."

For the first time since he had met the wizard Billy felt true anger rise up in his heart.

"Do you mean to say that I, and the others, have travelled all this way; we have lost Joseph, we may even lose Jack, and you do not know when you will be able to help us?"

Billy glared at the wizard.

The wizard, though obviously stung by Billy's words, remained calm.

"Why did Joseph have to die?" Billy was on his feet now and his sword drawn again.

"Joseph did not have to die," the wizard replied.

With his free hand Billy fumbled to get the pouch on his belt open; he took out the book and held it up in a shaking hand.

"Not according to this!" he shouted.

"The warning in the book was clear. All he had to do was heed it."

"Surely you could have done something to save him? You predicted that these things would happen!"

"No, that is not true," the wizard corrected. "I merely warned that they could happen. It was a terrible thing for me to watch Joseph die."

Billy who had become rather tearful during his outburst managed to regain his composure before asking; "What do you mean? Did you see the fight?"

"All the time I have rested within these walls; I have been able to travel without form. I have seen many a wrongdoing; I have only been able to watch and so often I wished that I had been able to help."

The wizard's eyes now showed the sadness he felt so sorely.

"Oh, I am so sorry," Billy managed to mumble, "it is just... he was my friend."

"I know, Master William. Sometimes the gifts I have seem more like a curse. The tired old body I had when I came here is now taking on the shape I had as a young man. I have gained new wisdom, but, as yet, I have no real power beyond these walls. I am safe here and once you entered the valley I hoped you would all be safe, even if only for a while. Cornelius would not have risked either himself or the lives of any of his followers here as he knows the great magic this valley holds. Any attack he made beforehand was to dishearten you. He knew that once here that any one of the others may turn on you and thus, his hold over Ildland would be sure again. Once you leave this place he will do his utmost to draw you to him. I will guide you as best I can. The hardest part of this war is about to begin, Master William, and the courage you have shown in coming here convinces me that I am right."

"Right?" asked Billy.

"Yes; right about you. I am right about you, am I not, Master William?"

The directness of the question required a direct answer.

"Yes," was all Billy said in reply.

CHAPTER FOURTEEN

"Come then, Master William," said Jeremiah, "it is time for me to meet the others. See to those bolts!"

Billy walked over to the door and found the first bolt, the one at the bottom now shifted with ease; it was the same with the top bolt.

"Master William!" Alicia exclaimed.

Both she and Luke greeted him with big smiles.

"What happened, Mater William? We were so worried. We did not know what…" Alicia did not finish.

Jeremiah had put a hush to her words when he became visible in the doorway behind Billy.

"Alicia, Luke, may I present to you Jeremiah." The introduction, although maybe a little grandiose it its tone, gave Billy the feeling that he had made up a little to the wizard after his rudeness on their initial meeting.

"Though, please, do not try to shake hands!"

Jeremiah laughed at Billy's hissed whisper aside.

"It is a pleasure to meet you both! Now, where is your friend Jack?"

The wizard glided past them to where he could now see Jack still lying on the altar.

Noticing the slight transparency of the wizard's appearance both Alicia and Luke gave Billy an alarmed look.

Billy gave them a reassuring smile and said, "I will try to explain later."

They all turned their attention to where Jeremiah was hovering, only very slightly above the ground, and casting a watchful eye over Jack.

"Please, Jeremiah, can you help him?"

Alicia's request was not answered audibly.

Instead, the wizard stretched out his arms so that his cape formed a veil around Jack.

The wizard held his stance for a moment and then slowly, much to the astonishment of the others, Jack's limp body began to rise from the altar.

He was approximately two feet above it when the wizard turned to face his young audience.

Jack landed back on the altar with a thump.

"Ouch!"

The sound of the disgruntled Jack on landing was music to his friends' ears.

"There," said Jeremiah, "it is done."

"Jack?" Luke was watching in awe as the partner he had feared lost was struggling to sit up.

"Where am I?" Jack asked.

The rush of the three to the altar would have knocked Jeremiah over (had he been whole) and their excited babble left Jack looking more than a little bewildered.

"Give the boy some air," Jeremiah requested. "Luke, you help him to his feet."

Luke did as he was told and, though he wavered slightly at first, Jack was soon able to stand unaided.

"How are you?" asked Luke.

"I feel fine. I – who are you, sir?"

Jack looked at Jeremiah, quizzically.

"This, Jack, is the great wizard Jeremiah," Luke answered by way of introduction.

"You were with me," Jack said to the wizard, "all the time you were with me. Thank you."

Jeremiah smiled back at him and then suggested that Luke should remove Jack's blood-stained dressing.

The wound had healed completely.

"I think," said the wizard, "it is way past the time you all should have eaten. So I will prepare food and drink for you all and in return you shall listen to my tales of Ildland past."

Prepare was not really the word, the wizard simply conjured up a veritable feast from thin air and, once they were comfortable, he started his marvellous tales of how the kingdom had once been.

CHAPTER FIFTEEN

Few words passed between Billy and the wizard over these next hours.

During his tale-telling Jeremiah had struck up a friendly banter with the others and had made them all laugh when he apologised for talking too much.

"It has been a long while since I was able to talk to anyone," he had said.

Billy somehow felt outside of the shared merriment, his thoughts more on the matters that were to be at hand.

When the wizard gave the order for the others to bed down, assuring them that it was quite late in the day, he spent a few quiet moments with Billy.

He took him to the altar where they had laid Jack down.

"Lay your hand upon the stone, just there," he instructed.

Billy placed his hands where indicated and a section of the altar pushed inward, and then came slowly outward forming a small drawer.

Before him, arranged carefully on a small cushion, was a neatly wrapped scroll.

"Take the scroll," said Jeremiah, "and put my book in its place."

Billy made the exchange ensuring he secured his pouch

afterward.

He pushed the section of altar back in, sealing up the drawer, leaving no trace of the secret compartment.

"That is good, Master William. Now, I must bid you farewell. I hope we may meet again soon."

Jeremiah drifted back in to his inner chamber and the door shut quietly behind him.

Although the wizard was no longer in the room Billy could feel his presence all about him.

It was a very comforting feeling.

"Good night, Jeremiah," Billy said, almost to himself.

****

The next day was to bring a strong sense of duty amongst the group.

After they had risen, Billy checked the scroll that he had been given in exchange for the book.

It was a map.

Billy placed it down between them so they were all able to see the course that Jeremiah wanted them to follow.

The course was clearly marked by a black line which was sporadically cut through with an "x", and a place name was written at each of these points.

"Do you know any of these places?" asked Billy.

"They are all a good way from our old home," Alicia said, "My father spoke of these places many times. Most were trading towns before the time of Cornelius. I gather that they are now either slave encampments or places where the followers of

Cornelius enjoy their sports."

"Sports?" Billy queried.

"Yes, sports. Many of those enslaved by Cornelius are either made to fight their own or to fight the knights. We have never made a habit of talking about these places amongst ourselves as it is such a sad thing to contemplate."

At this point both Luke and Jack nodded.

"It is rumoured, Master William, that all of the fights are to the death. Goodness knows how many have died for the entertainment of the knights and for the others who follow him."

"Then it is down to us," said Billy, "to put an end to the tyranny. Come! Let us make our way. We shall gather the good people together and take back the land that is yours and theirs."

The group got their possessions together, some supplies that Jeremiah had left for them, and then walked to the door that led them to the stairway down.

The door was ajar and once they had fully opened it and passed through it shut behind them.

They made their way down the stairs to the point where they had first entered the mountain.

"Goodbye, my brave young ones."

The sound of the wizard's voice cheered them all as the wall before them opened up and a chilly rush of fresh air hit their faces.

Once outside the wall became whole again.

Billy went to the rock where he had used the book as a key and found that the area was now completely smooth.

He smiled to himself.

Jeremiah had made it impossible for anyone to penetrate the mountain.

Billy got to his feet.

"My, it is misty," said Alicia.

The rest had to agree.

The mist before them was very dense, though curiously, stopped a few feet before the mountain.

Billy stepped forward.

"I cannot see at all beyond this. We had best hold hands and keep a straight line. We do not want to lose ourselves."

They linked hands, and made their way, cautiously, into the mist.

"Oh, this is horrible," Alicia said in a tone of dismay.

The boys all agreed with her sentiment.

"If we keep talking I think that we shall all feel better about this," suggested Billy.

So, that is what they did.

They talked about nothing in particular for what seemed to be a great many hours.

Then, with no indication whatsoever, they stepped out of the mist.

The first question that sprang to mind for them all was asked by Alicia:

"Where are we?"

CHAPTER SIXTEEN

There had been a few moments' silence before Billy responded to Alicia's question.

"I suppose we all expected to still be in the valley somewhere."

The rest of the group nodded their agreement.

"Well," Billy continued, "I think we have no choice but to follow the track we are now on."

The track ahead was lined with trees on both sides and ran as far as the eye could see.

"We had best use the trees as cover," Billy suggested.

"Master William," Alicia said; "look behind us."

The mist had gone; all they could see now was the same as lay ahead except for evidence that they had somehow navigated their way down a steep slope.

"Ssshhh!"

The order from Jack made the others jump.

"Quickly; get in to the trees!"

They followed Jack a few yards in and he motioned for them to stop.

They all crouched down.

Jack's voice was little more than a whisper when he turned his attention to Luke.

"Can you hear it too?"

"Yes. There are horses approaching. I think I can hear carts as well."

Billy and Alicia looked at each other.

Billy felt little comfort in the fact that she could obviously hear nothing either.

Jack and Luke had been right.

Soon they could make out the first of several knights coming down the slope.

"We must move further in," said Jack.

They crept further into the cover of the trees.

The first cart had now begun its slow descent down the slope.

It was being driven by one knight and at his side was another knight armed with a cross-bow.

"What should we do?" Jack asked.

"We shall track them," Billy answered.

Billy looked up at the sky.

"It is getting darker," he said: "it should be quite easy for us to stay hidden. We shall wait until the last man has passed and then follow. I just hope we will keep the cover of these trees."

For the second time Billy watched the type of procession that had made his blood run cold on his arrival in the kingdom.

Judging by the expressions on the faces of the others they had not seen the like before.

The prisoners shuffled, with heads down; their pallid faces made Billy shiver to the bone.

The carts clattered past; Billy assumed they were filled with supplies. Each one had a knight driving and another armed with a cross-bow.

It took some time for them all to pass.

"Jack," Billy whispered, "you lead, and Luke, you bring up the rear. I think Alicia and I both need you to aid us with this."

They fell into line and began to follow the procession.

For two or more hours they followed.

Each step they took was carefully planned so as not to crack down on a twig, or rustle any leaves that lay upon the ground.

The track led up another slope.

Jack indicated that they should stop.

"We must wait for a moment," he said in a hushed tone. "The cover is not too good ahead. We have to be very careful now."

They waited until they could no longer see the last knight who rode over the top of the slope.

"Come," said Jack: "we will soon break cover of the trees; the second we do, we must crawl on our bellies."

They took the remaining steps they could and then crawled up a grassy knoll to look down the track.

The track ran down to an encampment.

There was one very large hut-type building flanked by a dozen or so smaller ones.

They could also see a makeshift arena surrounded by knights.

The arena was lit by torches.

The new arrivals were herded in to the large hut whilst the knights who had come in on the carts began to unload supplies.

Two prisoners were ushered into the arena.

As far as Billy could tell they had not been amongst those in the procession. They were garbed in white tunics that stopped midway down the thigh.

The men in the procession had all been dressed in rags and looked as if they had travelled too far to be strong enough to provide entertainment for the knights.

The light from the torches around the arena made it almost possible, even from their vantage point, to see the faces of the men.

Women prisoners were kept busy by serving food and drink to the knights.

Two swords were thrown into the arena.

There was some movement to ensure that the arena was surrounded by four impenetrable walls of knights.

"Oh, no…" Alicia's voice became a hoarse croak.

Both prisoners picked up their swords.

One of the men tried to run at the wall of knights.

His attempt at escape was brought to an abrupt halt as one huge knight stepped forward and crashed his own sword into that of the prisoner.

He was sent to the ground with a swipe from the hilt of the knight's sword.

Two other knights beat on the felled prisoner with staffs whilst the other could only look on helplessly.

The huge knight hauled the dazed and bleeding prisoner to his feet.

His sword was given back to him.

The order to fight was given by a barked command.

Billy looked at the faces of his horrified friends, and then, under his breath he said, "You will be my first."

****

None of the group waited to see the result of the cruel contest.

The almost deafening cheers of the spectators drove them back under cover of the trees.

It was here Billy outlined his plan.

"We shall wait until the noise has stopped. Hopefully, we will then be able to see what the guard situation is. I would imagine that many of the guards will be drunk in their sleep tonight as I do not expect they were drinking water with their food. I think the best thing to do will be to move as one and take the guards on the outside of the camp first; then move inwards. We must get to the large hut to free the prisoners and with their help we will be able to take the rest of the knights; perhaps before most can even leave their beds."

"Do you mean that we should kill them all?" asked Alicia.

"Yes, I do. I believe Jeremiah wants this to be an important first strike against Cornelius. We have here a chance of surprise attack. I think we should cut as deeply as we can."

The group fell silent.

And, what seemed an eternity later, the noise from the encampment below was finally gone.

Each of them took a deep breath in an effort to muster all the courage they could, then crawled to the top of the knoll to survey the scene of their first real battle.

CHAPTER SEVENTEEN

"How many guards can you see?" asked Billy.

"Six on the outskirts of the camp and two at the front of the prisoner's hut," Jack replied.

"I think," said Billy, "that we should move round to the far side of the camp just in case there are more guards we cannot yet see. If we use the shadows the few remaining torches are casting we should be able to circle the camp before moving inward."

"We shall need Alicia's bow for the main part as I doubt any of us would much fancy a clash of swords with guards. Besides, we must make each kill as quiet as possible. With distance between us and the guards we stand a good chance of success. Alicia, how true can you make your aim?"

Before Alicia could answer Billy's question Luke interrupted, "Alicia's aim is the truest of all."

"It is," Jack confirmed.

"Good," said Billy.

Jack, as before, led the way.

The crawl down the slope was difficult enough, but Billy felt that getting around to the back of the camp would be made almost impossible, as the torches now seemed to be casting too much light and not enough shadow.

Jack, however, expertly guided them in to enough cover so that the first guard was clearly visible, while they were totally hidden from him.

They were behind a low bush.

Alicia slid an arrow from her quiver and lay flat just beyond the cover of the bush. Raising her bow, she slotted the arrow in place and, using a crossways aim, let it fly.

The guard was in mid-turn when it struck through the chain-mail about his neck.

Billy was sure that the guard had fallen with an almighty crash; in reality he had hit the ground almost silently.

They waited for a moment; nothing.

Alicia signalled to Jack and before Billy realised what was happening; Jack had broken cover, taken the guard's crossbow and bolts and was back.

Alicia and Jack exchanged weapons.

They crawled backward from the bush into much deeper shadow.

"This," Alicia whispered, "will keep an even greater distance between us and the guards. It can also penetrate armour at close quarters should the need arise."

And so, one by one, the rest of the guards on the camp's outskirts fell.

The group moved inward, using the smaller huts to shield them, though never passing in front of the doors, until they had the two guards posted at the front of the prisoners' hut in sight.

They were crouched in good shadow, but a clean shot at either of the guards would be difficult.

Alicia confirmed this fact.

"I am sorry, Master William; I cannot guarantee I could get two shots off quickly enough to stop one or other of the guards raising the alarm."

"Jack, could you use the bow?"

"From this distance…" Jack did not even finish.

"Luke?"

Luke shook his head.

The ground between them and the guards was well illuminated by a combination of moon and torch-light making it highly improbable that any two of their group could sneak in closer.

None of them had realised this from their original vantage point on the knoll.

Before they could contemplate any further the door of the prisoners' hut swung open.

The huge knight they had seen earlier in the arena appeared.

He spoke with the other two, and then they crossed over towards the hut the group were hiding beside.

They all pressed themselves up against the wall using the shadow to its maximum effect.

They heard the guards enter the hut.

For several minutes they did not move at all.

When Billy trusted that the coast was clear again he peered around the corner of the hut to where the huge knight was now on duty.

"Alicia, pass me the crossbow."

"Master William?"

"Alicia, pass the crossbow, please."

The rest of the group looked on with great uncertainty as Billy placed a bolt in its housing.

Billy aimed and fired in almost the same move.

Billy passed the crossbow back to Alicia.

"There, it is done," he said.

Alicia looked over to the prisoners' hut.

"But, Master William," she said, "the guard still stands."

"If he were to fall, perhaps he would have made too much noise. Now, come quickly," Billy said.

The three looked hesitant.

"Trust me. Come."

The group moved as quickly and as quietly as they could across the open space.

The guard had not moved at all, and it was only when close up it became apparent what had happened.

Billy's bolt had nailed the knight's head firmly to the door frame having first entered through the eye-hole of his helmet.

His feet were still in the standard guard position; anybody looking from a distance would have believed he was carrying out his duty.

Billy took the key that was on a large metal ring from the guard's hand and opened the door without a sound.

He then placed it back in the hand he had taken it from.

The group were in.

It took a few seconds for their eyes to adjust to the dim lighting inside.

The prisoners' hut consisted of just one room. It was flanked on each side by uncomfortable looking bunks.

A few torches were the only source of heat and the light for the prisoners, hence the room was both damp and cold.

Billy gave the orders.

"We must wake them as quickly and as quietly as we can. Jack, you and Luke wake the first in each row and then get them to help wake the others. Place your hands over their mouths to keep anyone from crying out and ensure the others do the same. Alicia and I will stay here to keep watch."

Jack and Luke took their opposing flanks and began to wake the prisoners as instructed.

It took several minutes for the task to be completed as the prisoners were both tired and confused by their rude awakening.

Once they were all gathered together Billy spoke quietly, but as authoritatively as he could, instructing those in front to relay his plan to those behind them.

Although the men and women who made up the large group initially found it hard to trust the ability of the boy giving the orders, they were stirred to action when Billy said, "Remember that Jeremiah is with us."

CHAPTER EIGHTEEN

Once his plan had been relayed the party split into groups and any available weapons were divided amongst them.

The women and those men weakened by injury were led to the nearest safe cover.

The others gathered up the torches that had formed the makeshift arena.

Once Billy was happy that everyone was in place he gave the signal.

Jack had tied strips of cloth to his arrows and now Luke was lighting the first.

Moving inward from the furthest hut Jack fired the flaming arrow in to its roof.

Luke followed him through the camp as arrow after arrow was used in the same fashion.

It was not long before the flames had taken a real hold and the first cries of confusion and anguish could be heard.

Thick smoke was now billowing into the night air.

Some guards managed to make it out of their huts only to meet with their deaths once stumbling through the doors.

Any weapons were taken by their former captives then used against any others who had made it out.

The bolts from Alicia's cross-bow thudded in to some; Jack took others with the bow whilst Billy and Luke used their swords.

Some horses bolted during the general mayhem, one even struck down a guard who could easily have been his rider.

"Luke, Jack, take some men and round up as many horses as you can!" Billy ordered.

There were few other guards that made it out; a lot of them would have been overcome by smoke in the close quarters of the huts.

Either way, all had paid dearly for their drunken arrogance.

It was some time before the flames and the smoke had started to die down.

Most of the party were now on horse-back, a few having to share.

Luke led a mount over to Billy.

"Master William, here is a fine stallion for you."

"It would not have mattered if you had bought me an ass for I have never ridden."

Those who heard this laughed heartily.

"Perhaps, Master William, you would allow me?"

Billy turned his attention to the smiling Alicia.

"Offering your help is indeed a fine compliment; were it not for your fine marksmanship we may never have won here tonight."

Alicia smiled again and climbed on to the horse.

Billy climbed, rather more ungraciously, up behind her.

The party cantered to the road that led out of the encampment.

They turned to look upon the carnage left by their victory.

The huge guard still gave the impression that he was carrying on with his duty; in sentry position, the key to the prisoner's hut still in his hand.

It was the only building left standing.

Billy turned to Jack who was close by.

"Burn it," he said.

As before Luke lit the arrow for Jack.

They all watched as the flaming arrow ignited the roof.

It was not until the whole building was engulfed in flames that Billy gave the order to move out.

CHAPTER NINETEEN

Those next days were a breath of fresh air for Billy.

News of the victory had spread and as they followed the route marked on the map they were joined by new recruits daily.

The next encampments were taken with relative ease.

Billy, who by now was riding well, would lead the sweep, slaying as many of Cornelius's men as the experienced warriors within his party.

Some chose not to join the cause for they were too afraid to face the wrath of the evil wizard. For most, however, the sight of the many dead guards and the taste of freedom gave them all the courage they needed.

They gathered supplies, weapons and horses and their numbers grew to the size of an army.

Some nights they would camp in the cover of woods, lighting fires to warm themselves by and Billy would hear tales of old Ildland exchanged between groups.

As he passed through the ranks, often with Alicia at his side, Billy would try to get to know as many of them by name as he could.

Billy had been accepted as a true leader and all were happy to have him sit with them awhile and listen to their stories.

Many of those he spoke with had been aware that one day he

would come and had heard that he was a great warrior who was able to travel between worlds to save those who needed help.

Billy managed to maintain his modesty, but tried hard not to shatter too many illusions.

He had grown wise enough to know that the feeling of strength and high spirits amongst them was a necessary driving force.

He would occasionally share a knowing smile with Alicia before moving amongst others to bid them a good evening also.

It was on one of those nights that, as Billy walked back to the fire he shared with his younger friends, Alicia asked, "Master William, is something troubling you?"

"Oh, no, Alicia, it is just…" he did not finish.

"You have been more quiet than usual," she said in an attempt to prompt him.

Billy looked at her.

In the glow of the fires she looked more beautiful than ever, her eyes an astonishing green.

For a moment he stood and said nothing.

Then Alicia reached out to Billy with both hands and clasped them around his.

"Do not fear, Master William, I know that there are still many things you feel you do not understand."

"You do?" asked Billy.

"Yes," she said, "I do."

The warmth of her hands seemed to take the chill out of the night air.

Still holding on to his hands Alicia said, "If you understand what my destiny is supposed to be then I think that you must also understand what made me come to you first."

With that she let go, and without another word they walked back to where Jack and Luke were preparing to bed down for the night.

Billy lay awake long after the others had settled.

Then, when tiredness finally got the better of him he fell in to a sleep filled with the most horrible of nightmares.

****

At a place not marked on Billy's map stood the castle of Cornelius.

And on this particular night from within the bowels of the castle there came laughter.

A piercing, manic laugh.

The laugh of a madman.

A laugh that would bring sickness to the gut of anybody unfortunate enough to hear it.

Cornelius whirled around the room in a fit of absolute delight.

The long candles placed all about the room flickered as he ran from one corner to another.

He came to an abrupt halt and rubbed his hands together.

"Oh, my, my, how sweet."

He stood before the open volume bound in black and gold that was on the table in front of him.

His eyes glowed red, a deep blood red.

"Now I know how to get you, brat!"

Each syllable whistled and hissed spittle out between his teeth.

"I am going to get you! I will destroy you bit by bit! I will suck you inside out and take your soul for mine!"

He threw back his head and laughed again.

The sound travelled way beyond the room, further than you can imagine any sound travelling.

It crossed vales and hills, passed through woods, then rushed down into valleys until it finally subsided leaving behind the kind of chill that only a real fright can induce.

CHAPTER TWENTY

Billy woke with a start.

His blanket was wrapped awkwardly around his body as if he had been fighting with it during his troubled sleep.

He sat up and untangled himself.

He was sweating heavily and had to take several large gulps of air before he was able to control his breathing.

He looked around him.

All seemed quiet in the camp; Alicia, Jack and Luke were sleeping soundly near his side.

It was just as he was thinking of attempting to sleep again that he heard the sound.

Although it was faint he instinctively reached for his sword.

He stood up, his sword already drawn and listened harder.

With the force of a gale, the laughter he had heard only once before, tore through the woods knocking him off his feet.

"Cornelius..." Billy barely whispered the evil wizard's name.

All about him his troops were waking up.

Billy scrambled back on his feet, his eyes darting back and forth searching helplessly for the invisible assailant.

Billy could now hear another sound – the flapping of great

wings.

"Arm yourselves!" he ordered.

The words were barely out of his mouth before the first of the creatures were upon them.

These were even bigger than those that had taken the children; they were even more hideous and each had a rider.

Now that his eyes had adjusted fully to the half-light about them Billy could make out the dwarves that held the reins of each bird.

All were armed with crossbows.

They were able to master the reins with one hand whilst taking deadly aim with the other.

Billy saw at least twenty of his troops go down with the first swoop.

The creatures then soared upward and hovered, allowing the dwarves to reload before plummeting down again.

Billy grabbed a bow for himself and with his first shot took a dwarf clean off its mount.

Again though, more of Billy's troops were struck down.

Billy was also aware of the fact that there were some in his army who were beginning to scatter.

He had little time to dwell on this as more of the creatures dived upon them, their riders taking so much glee in the chaos they were causing.

An injured creature hit the ground close to Billy's feet and with a swipe of pure venom he sliced its rider almost in two, and then plunged his sword deep into the belly of the beast.

Some of the dwarves who had been toppled from their mounts were engaging in sword-play with his troops.

Their size made them a difficult prospect on the ground, for though their own swords were small, their speed often allowed them inside of a missed blow to finish their opponent.

Others who managed to salvage their crossbows were able to despatch opponents before even being seen.

Billy fought on, with sword or any weapon that came to hand; he was taking more and more of the dwarves and birds alike.

It was at the point where Billy's fury was laying waste to so many that the attacks suddenly stopped.

The creatures had all flown back to the sky, so high that they all but disappeared.

"Oh, no…" this was all Alicia managed to say.

Way above them hundreds more of the creatures were gathering until they resembled a vast black cloud that almost eclipsed the moon.

Billy watched as more of his men had now decided that it was time to run.

He cursed, but in his heart he could find no way to blame them for their actions.

The camp was, in many places, piled high with the corpses of men, women, the creatures and dwarves.

The sobs of the women who had lost their husbands was the saddest of sounds.

"Those men who want to go, go now," Billy commanded, "Take all the women and act as their protectors. Take any injured too. Now, move quickly before they are upon us again!"

Billy turned to Alicia.

Before he could say anything she said, "No, Master William, you know I have to stay."

Jack and Luke held their ground as did thirty or more other men.

"We have lived by the sword many times," said one by way of explanation, "and, if deemed necessary, shall die by it."

"I thank you for your courage," Billy replied, "Now, let us be ready."

The creatures above them were starting to circle downward.

Billy could hear those who had decided to go crashing desperately through the woods trying to find deeper cover.

Looking up into the sky Billy took a deep breath and then gave the orders for battle.

"Spread yourselves out, we must make it as difficult as possible for them to get us; use any cover you can!"

There was no time to say anything else.

What was surely to be the final dive had begun.

The speed at which they came down was seemingly suicidal.

But, as each of the groups came down, so they were able to bank up just as quickly.

Their lethal hail of bolts thudded repeatedly into many of those who were already dead, though with each wave fresh cries of anguish could be heard.

Billy's army was almost depleted when he saw something that made his misery complete.

Alicia had stumbled onto open ground and was taken skyward in the grip of one of the winged creatures, its rider seemingly on a mission to get away as quickly as possible.

Any attempt to rescue her would have been futile, a shot from a bow could have hit her and if dropped from such height she would probably be killed anyway.

All Billy could do was scream.

"NO! NO! NOT HER! LEAVE HER ALONE!"

The attack halted.

The remaining birds took their riders upwards and in seconds were out of sight.

Billy looked around him, tears of dismay flooding from his eyes.

Luke and Jack had survived and perhaps another ten of his men.

At this point it was hard to tell as Billy was almost blinded by his tears.

His battered body could take no more.

There was a flurry of wind that would normally have preceded a violent storm, instead though, came the voice of Cornelius:

"Now, I think we understand each other, Master William!"

Its tone so deep, its volume close to a roar, it crashed around inside of Billy's head and totally overwhelmed him.

"No…" Billy mumbled.

He staggered and before either Luke or Jack could catch him, fell to the ground in a dead faint.

CHAPTER TWENTY ONE

Billy came to with a violent jolt, though he could see nothing.

But he could feel.

He was being sucked downward with great force.

His body and face were suffering the scratches of a thousand sharp, tiny stones.

His mouth, eyes and ears were filling with dirt.

He could feel slimy creatures wriggle about between his fingers and round the wrist of the hand that still clasped his sword.

The horror of what was happening dawned.

He was being dragged down through the earth!

His immediate reaction was to want to cry for help; he did know, however, that he could not do this as his mouth would fill with more dirt or maybe he would choke on a worm or slug or worse.

There was nothing he could do except hope that his breath would hold out.

The only comfort he had in all of this was the knowledge that if he were to die, he would die as a true warrior.

With that one positive thought in his mind he tightened the grip he had on his sword.

His lungs were at bursting point when he plummeted into open air.

Before he had a chance to see where he was his feet had hit solid ground.

The speed of his descent caused his legs to give way beneath him and to lose the grip he had on his sword; he heard it clatter down somewhere behind him.

He was lying on a cool stone floor.

He sucked down the fresh air around him and let his pounding heart slow.

It took a monumental effort to haul himself to his feet.

Instinctively, he looked for his sword.

It was only a few feet away, but the heaviness with which he had landed had taken its toll on his left ankle.

He found he had to drag his leg behind him to get to the sword.

He picked it up and then stood for a while trying to keep as much weight as possible off the injured ankle.

He was in a cavern of some sort.

From somewhere came a reasonable source of air and light, though he could not fully fathom out from where.

There seemed to be several exits running off the cavern indicating that it might be some kind of underground maze.

Billy limped toward one of the exits when he was stopped in his tracks by a voice.

"Master William! Master William!"

The voice had come from behind him.

Billy turned, his sword raised, to face the person whose voice it was.

He could make out a shadowy figure just inside the first left-hand exit.

"Who is it? Who is there?"

"Master William! Come to me!"

The direction from where the voice had come had changed.

He could now make out a figure in the first of the natural doorways to the right.

"Master William! Oh, come to me do!"

The voice had taken on an almost mocking tone of melodrama.

Billy felt the first beads of fear-induced perspiration pop out on to his forehead.

"Joseph?"

His voice was barely a croak; Billy was shaking from within.

"Joseph?" he repeated.

Billy so wanted to run, but he was unable to move.

His body was wet with the fear that had begun to take control of him.

This could not be true.

This could not be real.

From within the passage directly before him a white light glowed.

It grew in intensity until Billy had to shield his eyes with his free hand.

The light burst forth into the cavern, and as it did so, the same figure he had seen before became visible again.

Only this time Billy could see that it was Joseph.

He attempted to speak; no sound would come.

All that happened was that his mouth dropped open.

Joseph took a step forward.

Billy could only watch.

There was no real expression on the face of Joseph.

He drew closer to Billy.

Billy could feel the grip on his sword loosening; his arms hung limply by his sides.

Joseph was getting to within arm's reach, when the expression on his face did change.

It changed to one of surprise.

He lurched forward in a very sudden movement; and then fell to the floor.

Billy sprang backwards.

He looked to where Joseph lay.

The arrow imbedded deep between Joseph's shoulder blades was an all too familiar sight to Billy.

Joseph's face twisted upward so that his eyes could make contact with Billy's.

"Are you sorry too?" he asked.

Before Billy could answer Joseph's body began to age.

From ageing it went in to disintegration.

"Are you sorry?" Joseph managed to repeat.

It was the last thing he could say, as seconds later his jaw crumbled.

His eyes popping, his hair fell in grey tufts from his head.

"No," said Billy. "I am not sorry. I am not sorry at all."

The thing that had been Joseph convulsed violently before turning inside out.

And then, everything was as it had been.

Billy knew he had witnessed the blackest of magic.

The voice of Cornelius came to the cavern.

"Hmmm," it purred, "very impressive. You may make a worthy adversary yet."

Billy put his sword back in to its scabbard before replying to the taunt.

"For somebody who does not even have the courage to show his face to me that is hardly the greatest of compliments."

"Oh, such spiteful words. Still, I would expect anybody who had lost an army in a single night might speak thus purely from bitterness. You shall have your chance at vengeance, young man, for we shall meet soon enough. I have a friend of yours with me who, you can rest assured, is dying to see you."

Cornelius allowed himself a sinister chuckle.

"Follow the path before you, Master William. I have grown tired of waiting."

CHAPTER TWENTY TWO

Billy left the cavern as instructed.

His route had started with an easy enough incline though it was not long before it had become steeper.

As it got steeper so did the ceiling of the passage get lower.

His progress became slower. Then much slower.

Most of the journey now involved him climbing upward over very uneven ground in a stooped position.

His knees and palms were cut and every time he lost his footing he would lose just a little more heart.

Every limb, bone and muscle in his body was racked with pain.

He managed to keep going, for even if this was just another of the evil wizard's tricks, he would have to find a way out.

He had to save Alicia and he had to keep the oaths he had sworn.

Now, when he thought of his desire for revenge, it acted as a crop would to a horse.

It was a while later as he clambered over another area of jutting rock, amidst the surface of smaller stones, that he had to lie flat on his belly.

He could feel a cool rush of air.

Somewhere ahead of him there was an opening to the surface.

He wriggled along until he could see it.

The ground beneath him was becoming more like normal soil as he drew closer. Although this was a relief to his injured palms and knees, it also served to make him even filthier than he already was.

He had made it to the opening.

He rubbed the sweat out of his eyes and peered through cautiously.

It was night and the sky seemed to be totally devoid of stars.

After the close confines of the passage out, the cold night air almost stung.

He hauled himself some way out in an effort to see more.

The much softer ground at the foot of the opening gave way.

Its movement had been so sudden that he was unable to stop himself tumbling forward in an avalanche of grit and dirt.

He tried desperately to get some sort of hand or foothold as he slid headlong down a steep slope.

But it was too dark for him to see anything that he might have been able to grab and cling on to.

He carried on ploughing downwards until he had smashed into a pile of something that definitely was not soil.

The pile separated and clattered about, crashing around or upon him.

Albeit clumsily, he had stopped.

A wave of panic rushed over him when, from somewhere within the pile, a bare boned arm bore down its hand and its fingers clutched at his throat.

Billy thrashed about wildly.

He managed to get a grip on the hand and, to his amazement, it snapped off at the wrist with a sickening crack.

Billy lashed out with his other arm and cast his assailant to one side.

Still dazed from his fall he somehow got to his feet and drew his sword all in the same move.

The pile shifted, bone clacking against bone.

It was then that, up above him, almost as if someone had drawn a shroud from in front of it, a full moon shimmered.

Billy could see clearly for the first time.

He took a step back, a shock-wave of near hysteria shaking him both inside and out.

All about him, piled one on top of the other, were skeletons.

The skeletons of people as well as all kinds of animals, large and small.

They were to his left, right, in front and behind him.

Billy looked up to see that the slope he had tumbled down was impossibly steep.

He was in a vast pit and the looseness of the soil on the slopes about him made sure that there was no way out.

As the moon rose higher in the sky something had started to take shape on the plateau the pit was formed around.

From within an icy mist that was rolling its way down into the pit he watched as a wall began to build itself.

It built upward so high that Billy could not see where it finished from his poor vantage point.

A second adjoining wall now rapidly climbed skyward, stone upon stone, as had the first.

Slit windows from which glowed a blood-red coloured light, appeared in well structured lines across and down the walls.

Billy could only assume that the two remaining walls had built up in the same fashion, for it seemed the final detail had taken its place.

A double door constructed of a heavy wood completed the front facing wall.

The doors creaked slowly inwards and a moment later Billy could see a figure appear between them.

"I hope you like my humble home," the instantly recognisable voice of Cornelius rasped.

"Oh, yes, very impressive," Billy replied, trying hard to sound sarcastic.

The truth was, Billy was more than just impressed.

He knew that before him stood the hugest castle he was ever likely to see.

Despite its grandness though, the stench about the place would discourage any visitors.

"Come then," invited Cornelius, "I shall show you more, much more."

"How?" asked Billy. "The climb is too steep."

He could see no pathway up the slope to the doors.

"Fly, brat!" Cornelius snarled.

Billy was lifted off his feet and taken high in to the night sky.

He flew so high that he could barely breathe then was forced to whirl around before diving downwards.

The ground was hurtling up to meet him.

Billy closed his eyes.

A feeling of sickness rose in his stomach.

Was Cornelius just going to smash him into a pulp and let his body decay amongst the others in the pit?

With a vicious jerk he was hauled upward again.

In the next minutes he became increasingly dizzy.

For a moment he could see only sky. Then only earth.

He could hear the wizard laughing. A maniacal laugh he had grown to hate so.

He was brought to a sudden stop a few feet above the ground in front of the castle doors.

Then, like a puppet that had had its strings cut, he fell to the ground in an undignified heap.

Billy dragged his battered body to a standing position.

The doors were open, but Cornelius was no longer in sight.

"Come in." The hissed whisper was not the warmest of invitations.

Billy, his sword still drawn, hobbled through the doors.

He had no choice.

****

Once inside, something which Billy knew would happen, did – the doors shut behind him.

The light inside was a dim red.

The few torches that adorned the walls made his own shadow look as if it was something to be frightened of.

The room that he stood in was large and formed a perfect square.

Apart from the doors behind him there was no way out.

There was a single item of furniture in the room. It stood exactly in the centre.

Billy edged towards it.

In a simply constructed frame, which also acted as its stand, was a looking-glass.

As he approached, his looming shadow grew shorter and once before it, had all but disappeared.

Billy looked at his reflection in dismay.

His face was covered in grime and streaked with sweat.

His tunic was in tatters and exposed the many gashes and bruises about his body.

Looking at his state Billy was surprised that he could even stand.

His reflection clouded over and now, the jeering face of Cornelius was in its place.

In fury Billy raised his sword, swinging with all his might.

The glass shattered in a spray of shards.

As each of these hit the ground another exact copy of the looking-glass grew from it.

Billy was surrounded by a hundred grinning wizards.

In unison they all threw their heads back and laughed.

It was hearty laughter, full of scorn.

"What kind of trick is this?" demanded Billy.

"What now, Master William?" they all asked at once.

Billy turned a full circle, staring hard at all the images.

"Coward," he spat.

The laughter stopped.

"Perhaps I can interest you in seeing your sweetheart, brat?"

Then, there she was.

In the glass directly in front of him he could see Alicia.

She was chained to a wall, her body was contorted uncomfortably, her arms stretched outwards above her head. Her all too slender wrists hung limply through hoops that were bolted to the wall.

The array of chains would have been a grotesque way to have kept a grown man captive.

As if sensing his presence she managed to lift her head.

The cherry-red lips that had captivated him so many times were dry and cracked.

Her once beautiful eyes were swollen and shot with blood.

The tears that started to course down her cheeks stung his eyes as much as they did hers.

It was now Billy heard another voice.

A voice from within his very soul.

"Now, show your worth as a warrior!" it commanded.

The hilt of his sword had grown hot in his hand, though instead of causing him to drop it, his grip got stronger.

"NO!"

The sheer volume of his cry had changed the expression on the many faces of Cornelius.

If Billy had had the time to look he would have seen this change.

With one very fluid movement Billy dove headlong in to the glass that contained the image of Alicia.

The was no breakage. He was taken through the glass and emerged in the dungeon where Alicia was held captive.

Rats scurried for cover, his unexpected arrival having startled them.

There were two others in the dungeon.

One was a dwarf and the other a hideously disfigured old man with a vast ring of keys on his belt.

The dwarf ran towards Billy, his sword raised above his head.

Billy skilfully side-stepped the dwarf, then with both hands, plunged his own sword into its back.

He lifted the creature off its feet and watched with grim satisfaction as it slid all the way down the blade to the hilt.

Billy then turned his weapon downwards, the dwarf slid towards the floor screaming. This was followed by a deep throated cough, then silence as it neared the ground.

Billy stepped on the dwarf's back to pull his blade free – the drawf twitched a little and then died.

He glared at the old man.

"Let her go!" he ordered.

From beneath the cloak he wore the old man drew his own sword with a gnarled hand.

The speed at which he moved took Billy by surprise.

Their swords clashed. The old man lunged and Billy would counter.

They fought savagely for several minutes.

Both were sweating heavily and breathing hard when the old man made what would be his final desperate attack.

Billy saw his opponent's move, parried the swipe, forcing the old man's sword towards the floor.

With a semi-circular twist his own sword took the old man's hand clean off.

The old man howled, his face turning white and saliva spraying from his deformed mouth.

Billy put the point of his sword to the old man's throat, not allowing him to fall.

"Let her go!"

The old man held his injured limb in his good hand, blood pumping between his fingers.

"Give me the keys!" Billy demanded, realising the old man would not be able to do the job unaided.

They moved towards Alicia.

"Which ones?"

The old man did not reply.

"Which ones?" Billy raised his voice.

The fear in the old man's eyes told Billy that he was scared witless, but still he would not answer.

Instead he gestured at his throat.

Billy drew his sword back a little then sliced the cord that bound the old man's cloak at the throat.

The cloak dropped to the floor.

A badly healed scar travelled from one side of the old man's throat to the other.

The damage the wound hand inflicted afforded him a grunt or cry, but he could not speak.

"Point then!"

Between them they managed to unchain Alicia.

Once she was free Billy told the old man to take a step or two back.

"How do we get out of here?" Billy asked.

The old man pointed towards a narrow set of steps that led to a door.

"Lead us," said Billy.

The old man nodded, still clutching at his maimed limb.

Billy noticed a piece a bloodied tunic on the floor and said to the old man, "Pick it up. Wrap it round your arm. It may help."

The old man did as instructed then shuffled slowly towards the steps – he had no fight left in him.

Billy followed, struggling hard to keep Alicia on her feet. She was almost a dead weight and mumbling incoherently.

It took some time for them to reach the top of the flight of steps.

"Open it," Billy said as they approached the door.

The old man undid the latch and pulled the door inward.

A hail of bolts shot through the open doorway – on each contact the old man was carried closer to the edge of the open landing.

Billy buried Alicia's face in his shoulder as the old man toppled off the edge.

Billy was sure he must have been dead before he hit the floor.

This, however, did not stop him wincing when he heard the old man's bones crunch on the stone below.

Two dwarves stepped on to the landing turning sideways to face Billy and Alicia.

Their crossbows were raised and ready.

They indicated that Billy and Alicia should follow them.

Alicia had come round a little more now and was stronger on her feet – Billy held on to her arm gently and they followed as ordered.

CHAPTER TWENTY THREE

Once through the door they were surrounded by at least a dozen more dwarves.

One of them, who seemed to be in charge, said to Billy, "Put away your sword."

Billy did as he was told, begrudgingly.

He took Alicia's arm again and the group moved down the torch-lit corridor in silence.

After travelling through a few more such corridors they were led through another door.

In this dimly lit room there was a little table.

On the table there was a book, a large volume bound in black and gold.

Billy had no trouble recognising this book even though he had never seen it.

Just beyond the table stood a man; he was garbed in black and had his back to them.

Billy was sure that he was quite the tallest man he had ever seen.

They waited for a few seconds, and then slowly, with dramatic effect, the man turned to face them.

At this close range the cruel curve of Cornelius's mouth was very evident.

The smile on his face was not one of welcome.

"Ah, my guests have arrived. Oh, my, my, you both look so shabby."

Billy did not rise to the insult.

He held on to Alicia's arm and waited for the wizard to speak again.

"Well, you shall be cleaned up. If you want me to respect you as a warrior, Master William, then you shall have to look like one."

Cornelius tapped his teeth with a claw-like nail and then waved his hand in a gesture of disdain.

"Take them away."

The two were then frogmarched out of the room.

For a time they journeyed down another corridor, before coming to two opposing doors.

"Take the girl in there."

Five of the dwarves began to lead Alicia through the left-hand door.

"Where are you taking her?" Billy asked his hand moving to his sword.

"To meet some of the other guests we have here," the dwarf leader interjected. "You shall meet them soon enough."

Billy decided it was best to let them go.

He was completely outnumbered anyway and knew he would stand little chance should he attempt to take them all on.

He managed a smile for Alicia.

"I will see you again soon," he said.

"You boy, in here."

Billy found it rather objectionable to be referred to in this way by one not even two-thirds his height, but refrained from retort.

The room he was led into, when compared with the others he had seen in the castle, was quite comfortable.

There were two tables, one laid out with food, the other with a water jug and a bowl.

A small bunk was placed beneath a slit window; next to this was a chair which had some fresh clothing draped over it and, propped against its legs was a shield.

There was also a pair of sandals under the chair.

"You are to eat and get some rest." The same dwarf was speaking again. "You will be summoned in plenty of time for the contest."

"Contest?" asked Billy.

"We shall be back later," was the only reply Billy got.

With that the dwarves left the room, closing and locking the door.

****

Billy had eaten and had managed to get several hours' rest before he heard the door being unlocked.

He sat up on the bunk.

The dwarf leader was there again, flanked by two others.

"Prepare yourself; the master is waiting for you."

Then they all stepped outside again, this time only closing the door.

Billy got up and moved over to the water jug and bowl.

He removed his old clothing and began to wash.

He had intended to do this after eating, but fatigue had got the better of him.

Once cleaned and dried off Billy put on the fresh clothing.

Everything fitted as if it had been made especially for him, even the sandals.

This gave Billy the eerie feeling of having been measured up prior to the start of the contest.

Billy put on his own belt and sword before taking the shield.

He gave himself a quick once-over then walked to the door.

He stood for a moment, collecting his thoughts.

Taking a deep breath, to gain as much composure as he could, he opened the door and stepped into the corridor.

"Come," the dwarf leader said abruptly.

Billy did as he was told and fell into step behind him.

The other two dwarves followed on behind Billy.

They walked a maze of all too familiar corridors until reaching another door, though this was larger and heavier than those they had previously come to.

They went through.

Billy's immediate reaction was to want to go back the way that he had just come.

They were in some kind of vast banqueting hall.

Wooden tables ran almost the whole length of the walls either side of the doorway they had come through.

On one side sat every manner of grotesque creature imaginable.

White-haired hags rocked on their seats with totally unbridled glee, their toothless mouths being crammed with food and wine by the dwarves who served from the table tops.

In amongst the hags were serpents, rat-like men, hugely fat cats, six-armed creatures who took relish in using their every hand to gorge themselves.

Their squawking, shrieking, flapping and disgusting grunts filled the room with a crescendo of noise.

By contrast, those on the other side of the room sat in silence.

The children at these tables had no feast.

As he wandered further into the room Billy could see the faces of the children, including those he had seen taken what seemed like an eternity ago.

And it was not long before Billy could feel every eye in the hall was on him.

At the far end of the hall was the head table.

As he got closer he could make out Alicia.

The hall fell silent as Cornelius got to his feet.

Alicia visibly cringed when the wizard, who had been seated next to her, placed a hand on her shoulder.

"Ah, good!" the wizard exclaimed. "The entertainment has arrived."

At this his followers roared with laughter.

"Your lady friend is not feeling well it would seem. She has hardly eaten a thing!"

Cornelius hauled Alicia to her feet.

Billy could now see that her hands were tied behind her back.

More whoops of approval rang around the hall.

"Get away from my table," Cornelius ordered her. "You have the manners of a heathen!"

He shoved Alicia in the direction of the other children.

A couple of the younger boys helped her to a seat.

Cornelius clapped his hands.

"Make the preparations! The contest shall begin!"

CHAPTER TWENTY FOUR

The preparations did not take long.

The food was cleared away by the serving dwarves, though they did leave the wine.

Another smaller table was brought in to the hall and placed in front of the master table.

On this, there was a sword and the black and gold volume.

Cornelius took the sword.

"I feel it only fair to offer you a challenge," he said to Billy. "It would be very easy for me to destroy you with my magic but you are, after all, only a boy. So, I am going to give you a chance to prove your worth as a swordsman. Who knows? You may even win."

Cornelius's followers cheered.

The children made no sound at all.

Billy looked to Alicia.

She seemed even paler now than she had been when he first saw her in the dungeon.

She shook her head sadly.

Billy turned his attention back to Cornelius.

"You swear before all of these witnesses that you will fight me as a man?"

Cornelius nodded.

"Yes I do. Shall we begin?"

"Wait a moment," said Billy. "If you are to have no shield, then neither should I."

Billy walked to where Alicia was sitting; he used his sword to slice through her bonds and then placed the shield down beside her.

"Wish me luck," he whispered.

"You know I do, but this is foolhardy," she replied.

Billy held her hand for the briefest of moments and then walked back to Cornelius.

"Young fool," the wizard hissed, "now, you have no chance!"

"We shall see," said Billy.

They moved in towards each other.

"To the death," muttered Cornelius.

"To the death." As he said the words Billy felt the glow of the sword once again and an iron will began to course through his body.

The first swipe from Cornelius's sword crashed down upon Billy's so hard it almost took it out of his hands.

Everybody in the hall was already on their feet.

Cornelius came at him again.

This time Billy countered well, ducking under Cornelius's blade and sent a shock-wave the length of the wizard's arm with his own swing.

Billy swerved his way round the following flurry, moving very quickly and lightly on his feet.

Cornelius was becoming extremely frustrated, realising now that his apparent size advantage was actually working against him.

Billy's confidence grew.

The next attack from the wizard was even more furious.

Billy had to block both swipe and lunge and then, somehow, managed to get inside and jab Cornelius in the stomach.

The wizard looked at his own blood on the hand where he had instinctively touched the wound in disbelief.

In a near blind rage he hurled himself at Billy.

Billy dodged the wizard, causing him to stumble.

Billy's sword came down again slashing the wizard's shoulder.

This brought a cry of disdain to Cornelius's lips.

A murmur ran round the room.

The following clash was equally violent.

Billy went inside again, only this time, Cornelius spotted the move.

He whirled around and delivered a blow with his elbow to Billy's face.

Billy went down to a roar of approval from the wizard's followers.

Cornelius moved in for the kill.

Billy rolled away just a split-second before the wizard's sword would have finished him.

The wizard cursed and brought down his sword again.

Billy rolled this way and that, each time managing to avoid the blade.

The wizard had his own sword raised above his head when Billy seized his own opportunity.

Instead of rolling to avoid the sword of Cornelius he stabbed upward with his own.

This time his own sword sunk in quite deeply.

Billy then pulled back on his own sword and used his legs to take the wizard's feet from under him.

The second that Cornelius hit the floor the ever treacherous dwarves were upon Billy.

Their little fists pounded him about the head and body.

Billy fought back with his own punches, gouges and kicks.

The hall was in uproar.

Billy got to his feet only to find more dwarves ready to take him on.

Cornelius was also up and staggering towards the book.

"Kill him! Kill him!" the hags were shouting.

Billy heard their blood-lust as he did battle with the dwarves.

Billy could see Alicia was moving to intercept Cornelius.

She used the shield as a weapon, swinging it about.

She caught Cornelius fully in the abdomen and sent him sprawling.

The wizard, though dazed, got back to his feet and before she could effectively use the shield again Alicia was struck down by the wizard's sword.

The anger that had grown within Billy turned deadly.

With one bone-crunching swipe he despatched several dwarves.

He had to stop Cornelius.

He ploughed through the crowd killing any of the wizard's followers that attempted to halt his pursuit.

They reached the table simultaneously.

Their struggle was now hand to hand for neither had the

strength to raise their swords.

Cornelius clung to Billy in a last-ditch attempt to stop him getting to the book first.

Billy pulled the wizard in towards him and hit him twice in the face, causing his nose to bloody. Billy hit him a third time and he went down.

As he reached for the book Billy was aware of more dwarves coming his way. The odds were now mounting steeply against him.

His hand made contact with the book and at the top of his voice he screamed:

"JEREMIAH, DO NOT FORSAKE US NOW!"

Billy was thrown backwards as a gust of wind hit him harder than any of the punches he had landed on Cornelius.

The book flipped open, its pages flicking to and fro manically.

The wind whipped itself into a frenzy, and then homed in on the followers of the evil wizard.

Billy could see the frightened faces of the children watch dumb-struck as dwarf, hag and other creatures of horror were lifted off the ground.

They were whizzed round and round, their screams a symphony of terror.

Then, one by one, they were hurled against the walls, their bodies piling upon each other as they slid towards the floor.

"Stay where you are!" Billy ordered the children. "None of you shall be harmed!"

Billy dragged his own bruised and beaten body to where Alicia lay.

Blood was seeping through her clothing on one side and a dark crimson trickle issued slowly from the corner of her mouth.

Billy could see that her very life was draining away.

"Please, please, do not die."

She said nothing, but, just for a second, her hand gripped on to his tightly.

Then, her hold loosened and her hand dropped to her side.

"Oh, no…" Billy mumbled.

Before any real grief could take hold Billy could feel that somebody was standing over him.

Cornelius!

He turned around trying to get his sword ready to defend himself.

The wizard's sword was already poised.

"Too late, brat!" he snarled.

In his semi-crouched position Billy had little chance.

The sword was coming down.

It did not make contact, however.

Billy, who had closed his eyes, looked up to see Cornelius dangling above the ground; one huge hand had hold of his throat, the other had his sword arm locked out straight.

Cornelius looked like a child compared to the gargantuan figure of Jeremiah.

Billy got to his feet, his sword now ready.

"Finish him," said Jeremiah.

He dropped Cornelius in a heap on the floor.

Billy ran him through before he was even half-way up.

Cornelius's sword clattered to the ground.

"You gave me no chance," he managed to gasp.

"I never intended to," said Billy, giving his sword a final twist.

Cornelius had gone limp.

Billy pulled his sword out and Cornelius fell forward hitting the floor with a thud.

Even now Billy was still ready to strike another blow.

Jeremiah knelt down and offered his hand to Billy.

The hall was now silent.

Billy looked at the devastation all around him and let himself be drawn in.

He cried softly into the folds of the good wizard's cloak.

"You have done well, Master William," said Jeremiah.

"What of Alicia?" asked Billy through his tears.

Jeremiah gently pushed Billy away so that he could face him.

The good wizard's own eyes were a little watery.

"It was not her time," he replied.

His smile said it all.

Billy turned and his heart must have skipped a dozen beats when he heard her let out a small moan.

"Go to her," said Jeremiah.

Billy ran to where Alicia lay and dropped to his knees beside her.

He took her hand, once again feeling all of its warmth in his.

Her eyes flickered open.

"Lady Alicia," Billy said, sniffing back his tears.

"Master William," she responded, still a little dazed.

Billy helped her to sit up.

"Goodness, what happened?" she asked, taking in the scene around her.

Her eyes came upon the body of Cornelius; and then finally she saw Jeremiah.

The good wizard was obviously happy to see her again.

"It is all over," he explained.

Jeremiah got to his feet and gathered the children together; he then collected the book of magic from the table.

"There are better things to come," he said. "Now, it is time to leave this place."

The children surely would have cheered were they not so weary, but their joy radiated from within them.

Billy found this uplifting and said to Alicia cheerfully, "Jeremiah is right. Let me help you up."

She nodded and Billy gently pulled her to her feet.

The wizard took the lead, then the children followed whilst Alicia and Billy trailed behind.

As they followed Alicia kept hold of Billy's hand.

"Master William…"

Billy turned his attention to her.

She did not finish; she merely looked a little sheepish.

Billy gave her a warm smile.

"I know," he said.

They had left the hall and tagged along behind Jeremiah until they stood before two doors.

The good wizard opened the right hand one and said to the children, "Go through and wait. I will just be a few moments."

The children obediently filed through the door and Jeremiah shut it behind them.

"Master William," the wizard looked very sad as he spoke,

"you are to go through the left door."

He opened it.

All Billy could see was total darkness.

Alicia protested, "No, surely not. Not after all that he has done."

Billy said to her, although he did not really want to, "I have to, Alicia."

His heart felt as if it would break when he saw a single tear trickle down her cheek.

"I know," she admitted, then threw her arms around him, hugging him tightly to her.

Jeremiah let Alicia hold Billy for a moment or two.

"Come," he said; "we really must go."

Alicia took a step back and Jeremiah placed a comforting hand on her shoulder.

"Am I to return?" Billy asked, hoping that he already knew the answer to this question, though the time he spent in Ildland had taught him not to take anything for granted.

"If you are to fulfil your destiny then, yes, you must," the wizard replied. "There are many things that you will learn in your own world from which you will gain great wisdom; and that will always be your most valuable asset. Besides, I assume you would like to see Jack and Luke again."

"I would like to see you all again," Billy answered, and then asked, "What of Jack and Luke? Where are they now?"

"They are still in the woods where you last saw them. A small band of men have gathered with them. They are waiting for your return or word of your return. I will explain everything when I see them next."

"Thank you," said Billy. "Please, give them my best."

He offered his hand to the wizard.

Jeremiah took it.

"Goodbye, Jeremiah. Goodbye, Alicia."

Billy took one more look into Alicia's eyes; it was a look that he hoped would sum up all he felt and all the hopes he had.

He said nothing else before stepping through the doorway.

The darkness swallowed him up immediately.

He heard the door close and for the first time in a long time he felt like a frightened child again.

****

Billy stumbled around blindly for a minute or so, then was back in the alley again.

Billy turned and examined the wall behind him.

There was the faintest of outlines in the brickwork.

Certainly a door had been there once.

He was alone in the alley, back in his school uniform and noticed his school-bag a few yards away, close to one of the dustbins.

He raised one hand to his face to check for his glasses; they were the only thing missing.

Billy scooped up his bag and now remembering how his adventure had begun, he felt as if he might cry.

He had no idea how long he had been away, but was sure that there would be a lot of explaining to do.

Then he shrugged, deciding that even if he were going to have to keep his memories a secret, at least they would remain with him.

Besides which, only cissies cry.

And he was a hero.

Proof of this fact was a small book in his schoolbag that now had its text complete, finishing one great story at a point where another could easily begin.